DR. HOTTIE

JESSA JAMES

GET A FREE BOOK!

Join my mailing list to be the first to know of new releases, free books, special prices and other author giveaways.

http://freehotcontemporary.com

Dr. Hottie: Copyright © 2020 by Jessa James

All Rights Reserved. No part of this book may be reproduced or transmitted in any form or by any means, electrical, digital or mechanical including but not limited to photocopying, recording, scanning or by any type of data storage and retrieval system without express, written permission from the author.

Published by Jessa James
James, Jessa
Dr. Hottie

Cover design copyright 2020 by Jessa James, Author
Images/Photo Credit: Deposit Photos: alanpoulson

Publisher's Note:
This book was written for an adult audience. The book may contain explicit sexual content. Sexual activities included in this book are strictly fantasies intended for adults and any activities or risks taken by fictional characters within the story are neither endorsed nor encouraged by the author or publisher.

This book has been previously published.

DR. HOTTIE

I'm not a big believer in romance. I'm certainly not the type of woman to get drunk, meet a guy, and go to friggin Reno later that night to get married.

But Dr. Hottie himself, AKA Jack Stratton, changed all that. Even if it was all a lie.

Okay, so our relationship is as fake as a bad spray tan. It's all to show up our mutual exes, make them realize how much they miss us. Can I help it if Jack is so ridiculously handsome that simply being near him makes me blush? And when he smiles at me...

Maybe I should've nicknamed him Dr. Panty Dropper.

And I admit, part of me is head-over-heels in love with him. How can I not be when he keeps telling me we have to spend time together? We have to keep up the charade. We have to kiss in private so it looks good when we do it for show.

When my ex finally gets the message a month after our "wedding", I'm left with two options. Go back to the man who the whole town says is right for me... or gather all my courage and strike off in a new direction. A direction that includes a new future that Jack and I make, together.

1

If Addison Fuller could summarize her experience with drinking tequila, it would probably go like this: tequila gives you rug burn on your face, and a ring on your finger.

But to tell the story correctly, she would have to start from the beginning, before she'd ever laid eyes on Dr. Jack Stratton. It would go something like this...

Addy made a frustrated sound, and felt a little chunk of her worries slide away. As she wiped down the built-in bookshelves in the great room, she felt the weight of the past ten days melt away. Even the confrontation with Jeremy seemed like a distant memory.

Who cares if it was just last week? she thought.

"Additup," her dad sang from his La-Z-Boy, which was perpetually parked in front of the television. "Take a break! You're making me tired just watching you."

"Then it's a good thing you're in a recliner," she said with a laugh.

"It's a holiday! It's your day off, take a breather," he said.

"But then who would pick up after you and Kenzie?" she asked as she moved behind him with a duster and squeezed his shoulder.

He shook his head and reached for a beer. It was his third

one of the day, Addy noted. Drinking beer, yelling at the television, and scowling at social invitations was the trifecta of his life. He barely talked to anyone besides her and Kenzie.

"Where is Kenzie?" she asked, wondering where her sister had gotten off to.

Her dad just grunted and looked at the tv in front of him. Her fingers itched to pluck the beer can from his hand before he passed out and spilled it all over the living room rug. She resisted, though.

I'll just wait until he's passed out. It's not like he's going anywhere.

Addy had worried about the drastic shift to hermitdom after her mom had passed, but it had been three years now.

This is the new normal, she thought to herself. She couldn't believe there had been a time when her dad had worked eighty-hour weeks getting his restaurant started.

"What do you think of checking out the fireworks this year?" she asked, though she knew it was pointless. "Dad?"

She turned around, but he'd already started to snore. Gingerly, she pried the beer from his fingers and put it on the table.

Just in case she might awaken him with her cleaning, she took her chores to the garage. There was a major project she hadn't had time for, one that had been on her to-do list for over a year. Keeping the inside of the home clean had been the priority. As Addy began to look through the stuffed shelves, a box of binders shifted and nearly hit her head.

Carefully, she began to pull out the box. Her own handwriting pulled her back to the blackest of days, when she'd been thirteen years old. It was when her mom had first been diagnosed, and she'd started to track the signs and symptoms meticulously.

Addison clucked her tongue as she flipped through hundreds of pages of her neat handwriting. Her mom's entire life, from the day of diagnosis to the day she died, was right here in bright pink and turquoise ink.

"Red and swollen lymph nodes today," was scrawled on the

page in her ten year old cursive. "Doctor says it's usually not a sign of cancer."

Yeah, well. Sometimes doctors can be wrong.

Tears began to threaten at the corners of her eyes as she pored over the binders.

"What are you doing?" she asked herself. She looked to the recycling bin and for a moment had a surge of empowerment.

What am I keeping these for? But she just couldn't throw them out. Addy put the box back on the shelf. One day she would do it, but today wasn't the day.

Once again, the garage was left for another day. In the laundry room, she sorted the clothes and began a new load. Addy moved to the refrigerator and started to rinse out old bottles of expired condiments and toss takeout food from the restaurant as the washing machine rumbled away.

Satisfied with the clean fridge, with the shelves wiped down and only healthy, unexpired options available, she sat down at the kitchen island and started to go through the bills.

Just as she wrote a check for the mortgage, her phone buzzed in her back pocket. It was her sister.

"Kenzie, what's up?" she asked.

"Hey! What are you doing?"

"Paying the mortgage."

"Ew."

"Ew? I don't pay, we're all homeless."

"Whatever. Anyway, I was calling to tell you everyone's going to Dusty's tonight for fireworks! You should come."

"Everyone? Who's everyone?"

"You know, everyone who isn't a dinosaur but is of legal drinking age. C'mon, you never go out!"

"I never go to Dusty's, you mean. There's a difference."

"No, I mean you never go out! You always stay in, doing the bills or whatever. And what's wrong with Dusty's? Dive bars are awesome."

Addy sighed. Her big Fourth of July plans were to stay home and go to bed early, but Kenzie's enthusiasm was infectious. Besides, her little sister was right. She didn't go out anymore.

"Okay, okay," Addy said. "I'll come. What time?"

"Meet me there in like… thirty minutes after my shift."

"Thirty minutes? Is that going to give you enough time to drop the deposit off at the bank on the way?"

"Oh my God! You never stop! Yes, Boss Lady, I'll take the deposit."

"Be nice or I won't go."

"Okay, okay! Bye Boss Lady, see you tonight."

As Addy put the phone away, she was startled by a monstrous snore from her father. He timed it perfectly, right in conjunction with a ding from the washing machine. She switched the wet load to the dryer and began broiling vegetables for her father's dinner.

The crockpot full of beef had started to permeate the entire house. As she prepped a chilled salad and kept an eye on the vegetables, a jolt of pleasure shot through her when she realized it would all be done at once—the beef, the veggies, the salad, and the clothes in the dryer.

Addison fixed a plate for her father and put it aside to cool. Everything else she stored in Tupperware and neatly stacked in the fridge. Addy looked at her watch. One hour to get ready. That was more than enough.

"Dinner's on the table," she said loudly to her father.

"Thanks, Jan. Love you." It was the usual response from her father's beer-laced sleep, but her mother's name always made her wince.

She went through her closet carefully and considered every option. Jeremy would probably be there—with Shannon. Everyone went to Dusty's.

What exactly does one wear to show your workaholic ex that he's missing out?

She sighed when she found nothing besides work clogs, jeans and t-shirts. Addy padded down the hall toward Kenzie's room, and stopped short when she saw her parents' bedroom door open and the light on.

Her dad sat on the bed and absentmindedly ran his hand

across the bedspread. He'd slept in the guest room on a small twin bed ever since her mom had died.

Addy knocked softly at the door. Her dad smiled up at her.

"Your mom loved the Fourth of July," he said simply.

Her eyes immediately filled with tears. He almost never talked about her mom.

"Are you going out?" he asked.

"I-- I was going to meet Kenzie downtown, but I'll stay and keep you company if you like. Dusty's really isn't my thing, anyway."

He shook his head and looked out the window.

"There's a plate for you in the kitchen if you're hungry," she said.

He didn't reply and she tiptoed out of the room. It felt like an invasion on her part, like she'd stumbled into something sacred.

In Kenzie's closet, she flicked through the designer jeans carefully hung on wooden hangers and sorted by wash. She flipped through and picked out a distressed, skintight jean skirt. Then she paired that with a tight knit tank top with an American flag embossed in gold on the front.

No one will accuse me of not being patriotic this Fourth of July, she thought.

She slipped into Kenzie's navy blue ballet flats. Something was missing. She held her own gaze in Kenzie's mirror and released her ash brown hair from its high ponytail, letting it cascade down her back. That was better.

As she drove to Dusty's, she couldn't get the image of her dad out of her head. He looked so lost, so small in that room. Yet she'd understood that he wasn't being a martyr or stubborn. He'd truly wanted to be alone that night. It made her sad, though.

She had to park on the street three blocks from the bar. Even from that distance, she could hear the music as it blared into the night.

The bouncer, a quiet boy she'd gone to school with, nodded at her and she began to weave her way through the packed crowd. Most of them were local drillers and their families, vaguely familiar faces she'd seen at Target throughout her life.

Dusty's was packed wall to wall, but Kenzie was easy to spot. Her sister had scored a table, of course, an arm's stretch from the bar. Two pitchers of beer sweated on the table, and Kenzie was surrounded by people she'd never seen before.

"You made it!" Kenzie shrieked as Addy approached. She jumped up and hugged her tight. "Lemme get you a drink. Stella! Pour my big sister a drink. Here, I'll introduce you—"

Kenzie named a few people she knew, but two she didn't—Jack and Philip.

"And these two, they're the new doctors in town. And they both look like they just walked off the set of General Hospital," Kenzie said with a grin. She was already slightly buzzed. "Don't they look so young!"

They did both look like movie stars, Jack with his dark hair and dark eyes to match, Philip with lighter hair and an easy smile that lit up the room. They were both tall and broad, dwarfing Addy when they stood over her and shook her hand.

"I'm twenty-nine," Philip said with a laugh. "Hardly old."

"That's close enough to thirty," Kenzie said. "But most importantly, they're *single*. Be still, my heart."

Philip gave her a warm smile and a nod, but Kenzie immediately pounced back on him. He was skilled at this whole thing, and knew just what to do with a much younger admirer, Addison could tell. But it was Jack, the brooding one of the pair, that made her draw closer.

Addy had never been good at these kinds of things. She clutched her beer like it was a life raft and settled onto one of the recently vacated barstools. It was still warm from the previous owner.

She sipped at the too-warm beer and looked around the table. When she scanned back to Jack, he looked at her openly. She both smiled and laughed silently at the awkwardness.

"Oh, I love this song!" Kenzie said as Halsey began to pour out of the speakers. "Come on, let's dance!"

Philip jumped right up and let Kenzie grab his arm. Her

entourage followed suit. In seconds, the table was nearly empty, save for Addy and Jack.

"Looks like it's just the two of us now," he said.

The accent. Oh lord, the accent. It was Australian, and properly heartstopping.

"Are we really supposed to sit around doing this until midnight?" she asked.

He laughed. "I dunno. This is an American holiday, so you're in charge. But I think if we stick together, we'll be able to make it."

She blushed.

"I think you've picked the wrong American party leader," she said.

"Well. It might also help if we get tanked."

"Agreed. Do you like tequila?"

His eyebrows shot up, and even she was surprised at her own forwardness. But it was too late now. She grabbed his arm and dragged him to the bar. As soon as she stood up, the beer she'd sucked down shot to its full power. She was tipsy and emboldened.

"Four shots of Cuervo," she said to the bartender, a girl she recognized from high school. The bartender gave her the staple nod of the town, the one that said, "I got you, because we're in this thing together."

"I'll have the same," he called. Addy laughed.

She chuckled. There was no way she could drink all that and still be standing, but she would go along with it. If only to keep Jack looking at her like that…

2

"Cheers," she said. "But to what?"

"Well first, you have to make eye contact when you cheers," he said. "Otherwise it's bad luck. And second, let's cheers to a different reason each time."

"You go first," she said.

"Cheers," he said as he clinked her glass and held her gaze. "To American holidays. To your country's unabashed love of blowing things up, and pies made with Crisco."

"Nobody uses Crisco anymore," she said.

"Okay, then. Cheers because... honestly it's this, or I'll have to let Philip try to set me up all night."

She felt a small burn of jealousy go down with the yellow liquid.

"Cheers because I'm so fucking awkward," she said as she raised her glass.

"Hear, hear," he said. He made it look like it was Sprite he was shooting back. "Cheers because I signed a contract to be in this town for at least a year. God help me."

"Hey!" she said. "It's not so bad."

The second shot somehow went down even coarser than the first, and she pulled a face as she bit into the lime to cut the burn. From over Jack's shoulders, she caught sight of Jeremy and Shannon slow dancing as Paradise City began its first strums.

"Can't handle it?" he asked with a smile. "I thought pretty American girls could drink."

She blushed. *He called me pretty.*

"Yeah, well, I don't normally drink tequila."

"You ordered it."

"I ordered four."

"I know, so did I."

She gave him a look, and he grinned. She was nearly knocked down by that smile, so she raised another shot glass.

"Right. Okay, then. Number three. You ready?"

"Are you?" he asked.

"Cheers because my ex is here and it looks better to be talking to you than to be by myself."

"Wow, thanks," he said. "But I'll take it."

He downed the shot easily. "Why is your ex an ex?"

A laugh bubbled up from her chest.

"Uhhh… it's a long story. Basically he works all the time, and says he doesn't have time for a needy girlfriend. Except now he's with *Shannon*, I see him everywhere, all the time. Doing all the things he told me he didn't have the time to do. So…"

She ran her finger around the rim of one of the empty shot glasses, feeling an acute shot of jealousy burn through her. *Or is that just the tequila?*

"My turn," he said. "Cheers because what else do I have to do other than to help a girl get back at her ex."

"I'm not trying to get back at him," she said, too quickly. The taste of the tequila on her tongue made her cut her defenses short.

"Cheers because tequila makes everything better," she said.

It was true. As she took another shot, she felt the warm glow spread outward from her chest.

"How right you are," Jack said. "You're on a roll. Your turn again."

"Cheers because … it's better to be drinking than to be running everyone else's lives," she said.

He gave her a curious look. "Are you the mayor or something?"

"Hardly," she said with a laugh. "I work at a restaurant. I'm like the manager, but without the title or the pay."

"Ah," he said. "So you're the queen of your hive, then."

Briefly she wondered what he meant by that, but the tequila had started to turn her brain to mush. They slammed their glasses down on the table in unison.

"So you're a doctor. Do you love it?"

He ducked his head. "I do. I'm in emergency medicine, and there is nothing like the rush of adrenaline that accompanies helping someone who's experienced a trauma."

"So you do it because you're an adrenaline junkie?"

He grinned. "Partly. The other part is because my father was a doctor, and his father before him, and his father before him… so it was sort of expected that I would follow in their footsteps."

"Gotcha. You're fulfilling familial obligations."

"That may have got me into med school, but I had to pass the classes and work the crazy thirty hour shifts."

"I didn't mean to imply that you didn't earn the right to call yourself a doctor."

He nodded, raising another shot glass.

"Shot number four," he said. "Ready?"

"As ready as I'm gonna be."

"Cheers because … because … shit, I don't know." They both broke into laughter. The tequila had worked its magic. "How about we switch back to beer?"

"Oh, wow. Did I really outdrink an Australian?" she asked.

"I'm impressed. I figured you'd think I was British."

"Why?" she asked. She felt his arm at her waist as he directed her back to the table.

"Most beautiful girls hope I'm British," he said with a shrug. "Something about that accent."

Omigod, he called me beautiful. Either I'm really drunk, or he's interested in me.

"I don't like Hugh Grant," she said as she slid onto the barstool.

"Good to know," he said with a laugh. "So, tell me your sob story."

"What?"

"It's the Fourth of July and you're at a table with a veritable stranger. You have to have a sob story. Why are you here?"

"At Dusty's?"

"In this town."

"Oh. I was born here."

"I'm sorry."

"Hey!"

"I'm sorry I said it like that! I just arrived, I shouldn't make any judgment calls."

"It's okay," she said. She realized their heads were inches apart, but it was the only way to have a conversation with the music and the crowd. Somehow, it felt like they were the only two in the room. "Actually, I moved to Santa Fe for college as soon as I could. I couldn't wait to get out of this town."

"Why'd you come back?"

"I found out my mom was dead."

"Wait, what?" She saw the shock swim out of the buzz in his eyes.

"Sorry, I'm not good at this," she said. "I mean ... she'd been sick a long time. Breast cancer. But I ... I didn't make it back in time."

"I'm sorry," he said. "Truly."

"Thank you."

"I know how it feels—and I'm not just saying that. My dad died when I was thirteen. I was there, but I wasn't. You know? I was a kid."

"Let's cheers to that," she said, and they tipped their beers toward one another. "But you still didn't tell me why you're here. I mean really here."

He shrugged. "I was in Chicago, doing my residency. I didn't want to go back to Melbourne, so I came here."

"Quite the trip from Australia to Chicago to Tahoe City."

"Maybe. So you told me why you came back. You never told me why you stayed."

She sighed. "I came back ... you know, to take care of everything. And then I got stuck. There's no other way to put it.

I was taking care of my dad, my little sister, the whole 'estate' or whatever. Then ... I started dating this guy."

"Jeremy?"

"Yeah. How did you know that?"

"You said his name earlier."

"Oh, right. Well, we started dating, and I'd always had a crush on him since I was fifteen. He paid zero attention to me in high school, so when he hit on me... I don't know. I thought it was another reason to stay."

"And now?"

"Now he's with Shannon. And they're rubbing it in my face, even if they don't mean to. I don't know. Maybe it was a mistake to stay so long."

"Well, there's good news."

"What's that?"

"I'm completely comfortable with you using me to make him jealous."

"You are?" she asked with a laugh. "You seem pretty confident."

"I don't want to come off as arrogant, but trust me, Addy. I know what I look like. And I'm willing to use it."

"Wow," she said. "Better watch that humility. Don't want you getting low self-esteem."

He laughed. "It's just the truth. It's luck, genetics, whatever you want to call it. You should know how it is."

She bit her lip and looked into the depths of her beer like it held the answers.

"Besides," he continued, "you're way too pretty to be so concerned with him anyway."

She looked up at him. *God, he really is gorgeous.*

"What about you? Where's your family?"

He smiled. "Well, my mum is in Melbourne, sitting on the board of various charities. No doubt, plotting my marriage to some Australian princess who will be blonde and perky and easy for my mother to control."

"Whoa. That's... unexpected."

"If you were thinking that I'm an adult who has total

autonomy over my own life, you'd be right. But you also wouldn't be my mother." He sipped his beer and looked away, but Addy saw a flash of bitterness in his expression. "God knows what she's going to do when there are grandchildren in the equation."

"I'm glad that you ended up here instead of Melbourne. And that you're single."

He lifted his brows. "Thanks."

Addy flung her hand over her mouth. "The tequila is talking, more than I am."

He laughed, reached over and tucked her hair behind her ear. "For what it's worth, anyone who dumped you is a total jerk."

"Cheers to that," she said, and lifted her beer.

Somehow, another pitcher of beer arrived, but Addy hardly noticed. She was pressed against Jack's side as he showed her funny videos from med school. She showed him her Instagram, flipping faster past old photos that showed her and Jeremy embracing or kissing.

"I think your ex is going bald," he told her, pointing out several photos where it was beginning to be obvious.

"Fireworks!" someone yelled above the din. "The fireworks are starting."

En masse, the bar began to rush outside and bottleneck at the entrance. She felt Jack's hand on her hip as he steadied her. The blast of cool evening air shot across her face when they made it outside and she breathed in the Tahoe air.

"Over here," he said, and led her to an isolated spot beneath a staggeringly tall tree.

He wrapped his arm around her as the lights exploded in the dark. The crackle, the explosions, the excitement of the night—it all came to a head in her as she looked up at him. His eyes slid toward her mouth and she braced for a kiss, but something stopped her.

"Hey. What if... what if we pretend to date?"

He blinked. "What?"

"Just listen. I'm trying to make my ex jealous, you have your mom breathing down your neck about settling down with someone…"

He looked at her face, scanning it for something. She felt like her honesty was being gaged, more than anything.

"Just try it out! You know. We'll see—"

Jack leaned down and kissed her, sure and strong. *God, he tastes good.*

As he began to pull away, she fluttered her eyes open. Jeremy stared at her from the corner of his eye. He looked nonplussed, even with Shannon's arm wrapped around his waist.

Well, good!

"How'd I do?" Jack asked. "Think he's mad?"

"You want another drink?" she asked with a smile.

"Sure."

She led the way into the bar with Jack's hand in her grasp.

"Another round of tequila!" she called. The bar was almost empty as the rest of the revelers stayed outside for the show.

"You got a ride home, Add?" the bartender asked.

It was the last thing she remembered.

3

Jack squinted against the bright morning light. It poured into the room and lit up the unfamiliar bed. The strange sheets that smelled of vanilla.

Shit. It wasn't the first time this had happened.

For him, there was a fine line between really tipsy and drinking so much that he didn't remember.

You'd think after thirty years of life—and fifteen years of drinking—you'd figure it out.

His head roared. It wasn't the first time he'd been blackout drunk, but it was the first time in a couple of years.

He shifted under the duvet and realized he was at least wearing boxers. But nothing else. Jack glanced around the room, mostly white with a distressed vintage dresser in the corner. The back of a propped-open laptop revealed a yoga sticker and outline of California.

At least I'm still in Tahoe City, he thought.

But something seemed off. The entire room glistened like a gem. It took him a moment to realize it was glitter, all over the place. By some miracle, he recognized his phone on the bedside table.

Please don't be dead, he thought. There was fifteen percent battery and a string of angry texts from an unknown number. As he rolled away, he jumped at the sight of the half-dressed girl beside him.

Addison. Addy. It all came back to him in a rush, like being smacked in the face by a wave of memories.

He remembered being at the bar. He remembered talking and flirting with Addison, that it soon crossed the line into taking shots and full on hitting on her. But that didn't explain what they were doing *here*, or where *here* was. He looked her over for clues.

She was sprawled out on her back, her head turned to the side and her long hair covering her face. One pale pink nipple had slipped out the top of her bra. He felt himself harden at the sight of her full breasts. These were curves he didn't remember.

But he pushed the thought aside and pulled the blanket up to cover her. She didn't budge, and her breathing remained deep and heavy.

Jack pushed himself up, shaded his eyes, and looked around the room. Where the hell were they? He'd thought it was her bedroom, but upon closer inspection he realized by the frosting-pink décor it was more like a hotel. They were surrounded by several empty bottles of champagne.

That explains why I'm so goddamned hungover.

Jack lurched from the bed and staggered to the bathroom. As he leaned his hand against the wall over the toilet and started to relieve himself, he glanced down and nearly pissed all over the place. On his left hand was a shiny titanium ring.

Jack pulled it off and started to inspect it.

"Oh, no," he said. "No, no, Jesus, no." He raced back into the bedroom and reached under the covers for Addison's hand.

She groaned into the room. "What are you doing?" she asked, still half-asleep.

"Wake up, I need to see your hand."

"What's wrong with my hand?" she asked groggily. "No, it's my head that hurts—"

"We have bigger things to worry about." He finally found her hand and felt the cool metal on her ring finger. His heart dropped into his stomach.

"What is this?" he asked, and held her hand up to her face.

"Shh! Oh my God," she murmured and pulled the pillow over her face.

"Look, you've got to help me out—"

Addison sat up.

"Oh, God," she said, and jumped out of the bed. He watched her as she raced to the toilet in nothing but her underwear. Violent retching and vomiting sounds came from the bathroom, and his doctor training took over.

Jack grabbed a couple of towels, her hair tie from the bedside table, and filled a glass of water.

"Vomiting is good," he called to her. "Get it all out."

"I don't feel so good," she said when she had eventually gotten it all out of her system.

She emerged from the doorway, one of the hotel bathrobes wrapped around her slender frame. She looked like a child playing dress-up.

"I'm right there with you," he said. "Come here, sit down."

He arranged a comfortable spot on the chaise lounge and pushed the water into her hand. She mildly pushed him away as he pulled her hair into a ponytail, but he tsked until she relented.

"Sorry I puked," she said, sheepish.

"I work in the ER. A little vomit doesn't really bother me," he said.

As he looked at her with her bloodshot eyes and dark circles underneath, he couldn't help but feel sorry for her. Of the two of them, she clearly got the worse end of the bargain.

"You want to stay sitting up?" he asked. "Or go back to bed?"

"Back to bed," she said.

He tucked her in and went to the bathroom to refill the water. As he filled the glass, he took a second to himself. He looked at the gold band on his fourth finger of his left hand, held it up a little to examine it.

The fact that he'd had a wedding, that he'd blown through another milestone in his life without any attention paid, made him feel sad. Not that he'd always imagined getting married or anything. That was more his mother's obsession.

But every major milestone that he passed was just another without his father, the only parent that had genuinely cared for him. Yeah, his father could be a hard master, punishing Jack mercilessly for even the smallest failure.

But looking at himself now, Jack could see why his father had rode him so hard. He just wanted Jack to be successful.

The glass overflowed, and Jack was pulled from his thoughts. When he returned, Addy had rolled herself up in the blanket like a burrito.

"Addison?" he asked, but was answered with more heavy breaths.

His phone rang and she groaned in annoyance. He didn't recognize the number.

Fuck, I'm supposed to start at urgent care today. It was the hospital, it had to be. Jack searched for an answer, a believable excuse. But for the first time in his life, he had nothing.

Philip. Philip will know what to do.

He let the call go to voicemail and immediately called Philip. As he searched for how to start the most awkward conversation of his life, he stepped onto the small patio.

"Congrats, mister married man!" Philip crowed into the phone.

He pulled the phone farther away from his ear and winced. "What?"

"Didn't you get married last night?"

"I ... I think so?"

"Yeah, you were really trashed last night. I told you that Reno was too far to go—"

"Reno?"

"Yeah, I tried to tell you, but you and Addy were insistent. Don't you remember? I put you guys in a taxi and gave that guy a generous tip. A really generous tip."

"What ... what about today's opening? The new hospital? I was supposed to be there—"

"Oh, man, nobody even knows we're open. Don't sweat it if you don't make it here."

Jack rested his head in his hands. "Yeah, okay."

"How's Mrs. Stratton?"

Mrs. Stratton? Oh, he means Addison. Jack sat up straight and peered through the glass to the blanket burrito.

"Uh ... she's not really up yet. Listen, what exactly happened? Last night?

"You don't remember anything?" Philip sounded incredulous.

"I remember doing shots," he said slowly. "And looking at her ex's Instagram. Then... nothing."

Jack heard a click.

"Hey, buddy, I'll have to call you back," Philip said.

Jack looked at his phone, silent and close to dead. Slowly, he got up from the wrought iron chair and headed into the bathroom. Under the warm spray of the shower, he started to feel better.

By now, it was clear Addison wasn't getting up anytime soon. He called for room service as he toweled off and slipped into the same clothes he wore last night. They reeked of alcohol.

The food arrived fast and artfully arranged, complete with a rose in a vase. He tipped the attendant at the door and wheeled the cart in himself.

"Food?" Addison asked as he began to uncover the dishes. She peered curiously at the tray.

"This first," he said, and handed her one of eight Gatorades he'd ordered. She opened it and downed the entire bottle in a few gulps. After her second bottle, Jack offered her some of the food.

She scooted to the end of the bed, still partially wrapped in the blanket and began to eat the French toast, dry, with her fingers. Midchew, she looked at him.

"Are we in Reno?"

"Yep," he said as he tore into an omelet himself.

"Oh, God. Did we ..." she looked down at the wedding band on her finger. "Whose idea was it to get married?"

"Your guess is as good as mine."

"Oh, no. No," she said, and struggled to get up. She still held the mass of blankets around her. "Where are my clothes? Wait, did we ... we didn't ... *consummate* it, did we?"

"I don't think so," Jack said honestly. "I didn't, you know, see any evidence of that."

"Oh, thank God. Here's my shirt," she said. "I mean, don't get me wrong. You're hot as hell, but ... we just met."

"No offense taken. I think your jeans are balled up in the corner there. And by the way? I think we should be a little more concerned about the fact that we apparently got married drunk instead of thinking about whether we had sex drunk."

"You're probably right," she said. She balled the clothes up in her hand and headed into the bathroom.

Jack listened to the shower turn on and started to think about how to get the marriage annulled.

That was a thing, right? In Nevada? It happened all the time, didn't it?

"Hey, is this your laptop out here?" he called.

"I don't know. What does it look like?" her voice was muffled by the water.

"Silver with a yoga sticker."

"Yeah, that's mine. Apparently, I was Type-A planner enough to get that out of the trunk before getting hitched to a stranger."

The laptop was at two percent and had started to shut down. Still, he caught a glimpse of Jeremy's Instagram page before the screen flickered to black.

Addison slunk back into the bedroom, her hair wrapped in a towel.

"Feel better?" he asked.

"A little. I threw up the French toast, though. I ... I should have known better than to drink tequila."

"I hate to say this, but ... I think we should head back to Tahoe," he said. "We can, you know, figure out the legalities later."

"Right," she said, and nodded. "That's probably for the best."

He could smell both of them as they huddled into the small elevator. Outside, the sun was blinding and painful. They both groaned and shaded their eyes, neither of them with sunglasses.

"How did we get here?" she asked as they surveyed the empty parking lot.

"I think a taxi," he said.

"So we're stranded?"

"So it appears."

She sighed and trudged forward, and he followed her.

4
___

*A*ddy slammed her hand across her phone when the alarm started at five in the morning. She and Jack had just made it back to town five hours ago, after they both realized they'd lost their credit cards. They got the hotel's help tracking down a phone charger, and then wrangled an Uber.

She'd been energized on sheer adrenaline yesterday, but now reality started to sink in. Addy texted both Dawn and Kenzie, though Kenzie was just down the hall and wasn't scheduled for her shift until lunch.

I can't make it in today, she wrote. *Not feeling well. Dawn, can you handle all the opening tasks? Kenzie, please get there early if you can.*

Addy pushed the phone away and pulled the pillow over her head. She'd never called in sick for work in her life.

When the Uber had dropped her off at her car in the deserted Dusty's parking lot, she didn't even say goodbye to Jack. She'd just climbed into her car, dog-tired, and drove home. She was mostly thankful that her dad was already passed out and Kenzie was nowhere to be seen.

She heard the buzz of a text but couldn't bear to look.

They'll just have to handle it one day on their own, she thought as she crawled out of bed to fill a water bottle from her en suite bathroom.

Addy fell back asleep until noon. When she finally awoke, she was acutely aware of the awkward weight on her ring finger.

She couldn't believe that she had gotten drunk enough to get married the night before. She was always so on top of everything, so prepared. And of all the people to pick, she had chosen Jack, a veritable stranger. What had she been thinking?

Sure, he was handsome. Beyond handsome. And he paid attention to her. She remembered him calling her beautiful at the bar, remembered how hard she'd blushed.

But now she had to extract herself from a marriage. The thought of taking off the ring, of the fact that it would mean that she'd be invisible once more, hit her hard.

I have set myself up to fail, it looks like.

As she pulled on a clean pair of denim shorts, she pried off the band and put it in her pocket.

You'll have to deal with Jack and the whole annulment thing today one way or another, she thought. *No point waiting around.*

It was barely noon, and already she was soaked in guilt. From calling in sick to putting off tackling the Jack marriage situation head-on, this was the most procrastination she'd ever indulged in. It didn't feel good.

You can do this, she thought. *If you can handle Mom's death, Dad's alcoholism, the restaurant ... you can handle this.*

There was just one problem. She realized she didn't even have Jack's number or know where he lived. *But you do know where he works.*

It was hard to miss the sparkly new hospital located right off the interstate. It was the first new building in that part of town in years, and she'd been blinded by the shine of sunlight off its glass walls for weeks.

After she showered, she started to blow out her hair for the first time in months. Even as she spent extra time grooming, swiping on her good mascara and digging out Kenzie's old MAC lipstick she'd borrowed last month, she tried not to think about why she was trying so hard.

What are you supposed to wear for an occasion like this? she thought. There weren't any tips in Cosmo about proper attire for an annulment discussion with a total stranger.

She popped an ibuprofen from the glove box as she drove to the hospital. This was, by far, the worst hangover of her life. Addy just wasn't sure how much of it was pure hangover and how much of it was shame.

As she walked through the doors, she scanned the area for Jack. Several people she vaguely knew, all locals, said hello and looked at her speculatively.

Do they know, or am I being paranoid? Does the whole town know?

"Addison! How are you doing, baby?" A short, squat woman rushed toward her.

"Mrs. Koppel, hi. I'm alright."

"How's your father doing?" Addy had placed her as the former librarian from her own elementary school days, but she hadn't seen Mrs. Koppel since she was a kid.

"He's alright."

"That's good to hear." Mrs. Koppel glanced down to Addy's ring finger. Although it was bare, she instinctively shoved her hands in her pockets. Her fingers felt the brush of the metal at her fingertips.

"Can I help you?" She was thankful for the low voice and an excuse to turn away from the old woman's prying eyes. A young nurse stood before her. "Are you looking for someone?"

"Hi, yeah. Is Jack working today? Jack ... Stratton? I think?"

He glanced at Mrs. Koppel. "Dr. Stratton's in the ER. Just head down the hall there and to the right. You'll see the sign. Mrs. Koppel, you're still here? Is there something else you need?"

"Thanks." She gave him a grateful smile and rushed down the hall.

As she stepped into the ER, she was immediately engulfed in the trauma. Through the separate glass doors of the ER entrance, she saw Jack astride a patient on a gurney. His baby blue scrubs were wrinkled and stained, and he leaned over the patient, doing chest compressions. Jack barked orders she couldn't comprehend to the people who buzzed around him.

Addy pressed herself against the wall as the entire affair rode by her. Suddenly their little situation didn't seem so dire. The massive waiting room of the ER was filled with people whose eyes brimmed with fear and pain.

Somewhere in the opposite corner, a woman sobbed, the animalistic noises becoming a soundtrack for the room.

Jack caught her eye as he passed. For a second, he faltered and she felt an electric fire between them. It was over in a second, but left her breathless.

"Move!" Addy jumped at the sound.

From the opposite direction, a stunning blonde in purple scrubs rushed past her and Addy again flattened against the wall. The blonde doctor bent down over a boy with an obviously broken leg. His father screamed over him.

Addy caught a glimpse of bone, snow white and glistening, that protruded from the boy's calf. Although the boy's cheeks were streaked with tears, he no longer cried. He simply sat in shock.

Jack was gone, but as Addy swept her gaze across the room, she saw a familiar face. Philip headed toward the blonde and the young boy, who was being lifted onto a bed in a small curtained area.

Geez, he's gorgeous, too. Is being insanely hot a requirement for employment here? Stop it, Addy. You're already married.

She shook her head and walked toward Philip.

"—get the splint started. Mr. Holton, if you'll follow Nurse Bostian here, he'll get the paperwork—Addy. Hi!" he said as he saw her approach.

His face lit up as the nurse ushered the father away. "It's good to see you survived the wedding night."

She could have sworn the blonde doctor shot her a look, but she wasn't certain. After all, it seemed like the whole town had their eyes on her.

"Er, yeah—"

"Jack said you hadn't got out of bed yet. He'll be glad you're up and about."

"He did? He will? How did he ..."

Philip looked at her oddly. "Uh, yeah. Everyone around here has been dying to meet the woman who ensnared Dr. Stratton. He's a hot commodity, you know. Handsome young doctor, small town. Well, actually they weren't *dying* since nobody really knows him around here. But then after he charmed them all with some stories from your wedding night, and bam! You hooked him, alright."

"That's me," Addy said awkwardly. "I'm magic."

The blonde stood up straight and squared off with Addy, though she kept a hand on the boy's shoulder.

"Addy, you'll be glad to meet someone from Jack's past. This is Rosalie Crane. Rose, meet Mrs. Stratton! Also known as Addison."

Before either woman could react, Philip reached out and gently pushed her toward Rosalie.

"Hi," Addy said and held out a hand. "I'm, um ... how do you know Jack again?"

"I'm Jack's ex-girfriend," Rosalie said with a frown. "We went to med school together."

"Oh. Um..."

Jack entered the main room from the trauma area and pulled off a gown and mask. He stopped short at the sight of Rosalie and Addy side by side. Quickly, he made a beeline for Addy.

"Hey, the man of the hour! I was just telling these two—" Philip started, but fell silent when Jack grabbed Addy tight and bent her backward for a kiss.

"Ew!" Addy could hear the young boy say from somewhere behind her, but there was too much fire between them to stop.

"Please just go with it," Jack whispered in her ear before he pulled her back up.

She was too shocked to say anything.

"You must have finally climbed out of *our* bed!" he exclaimed. "I was worried I'd worn you out permanently."

She blushed and saw both Philip and Rosalie give him startled looks. Addy worked her face into something close to neutral, though she worried that her heart pounded so loudly the entire ER could hear it.

"Hey, where's your ring?" Jack asked.

She bit her lip and dug it out of her pocket. Addy held it out like an offering, flat in her palm.

"I told you not to worry about damaging it, darling. People want to see it on you!"

Addy blinked and obediently put the ring on her finger. It was strange to have a virtual stranger do something so ... personal. Command something so intimate.

Jack grabbed her hand and extended it out to Philip and Rosalie, along with a few nurses who had gathered around the commotion to see. Addy heard the oohs and aahs all around them, but it was Rosalie's deadly gaze that held her attention. Rosalie blanched, then made an excuse and fled.

Addy felt like she'd done something hurtful to Rosalie, even though she'd only just met the woman.

"Hey! What about my leg?" the boy cried after Rosalie, and a nurse immediately began to tend to him.

Addy searched Jack's eyes.

"Can I talk to you a minute? Privately?" she asked.

"Ooh!" one of the nurses said, and made kissing noises in their direction. "Stratton's got dibs on christening the new break room, I think."

Jack took her hand and led her to a private, curtained room that was empty. He perched on the small bed with paper sheets that crinkled beneath him. "What's up?"

"What's up? What happened to dealing with the legal stuff when we got back?"

"Well, hello to you too, love. That plan went out the window when I thought about it a bit."

"I'm sorry. What?"

"I was working on this guy who came in with chest pains, and the idea struck me. We should stay married for a bit."

She gaped at Jack, who smiled at her expression.

"Hear me out," he said. "My mum has been breathing down my neck, wanting to partner me with some dimwitted blonde. In this deal, I get to say, "Sorry mum, I've been married, it's all been arranged". Which will both delight me, and relieve me of some of my mother's expectations."

"Okay but… where does that leave me?" she said, confused.

"You get to show your ex how wrong he was when he ignored you. I will make sure that he realizes what a mistake he's made. This was your idea, after all!"

"Jack, I was drunk. We were both drunk. And besides, I meant that we should pretend to date, not get married!"

"Keep your voice down, people might hear."

"Right. Anyway, we can probably annul—"

"No, no. We have to stay married for a while. I'm thinking … two, maybe three months."

"*What?*" Addy crossed her arms over her chest and started to vehemently shake her head. "No. You're crazy!"

"Just think of it! I'm not the only one getting something out of this little arrangement. Imagine how miserable we can make Jeremy. So much PDA in public… And my mum will look at pictures of us together, and get so angry…. I'm sure the vein she has in her forehead will pop out."

He had her there. It was insane, but the damage was already done.

What difference does it make if we're married two days or two months? An annulment is still an annulment.

"Okay, how about this?" Jack asked as he considered the frown on her face. "You stay married to me for two months, I take care of the annulment, and you don't do anything."

"Oh! I don't know …"

"Addy, the hard part is done! We're already married. All you have to do is stay married to me for two months. I promise it's not that much of a hardship. I'm not that bad, alright?"

But if it sounds too good to be true…

Jack grinned at her. "C'mon. I'll even help you move after my shift."

"Help me … what? Move?"

"Well, yeah. If this is going to work, we have to look married. And married people live together. Unless you'd prefer I move in with you?"

A rush of panic flooded her. The idea of Jack even meeting her father was enough to put her in a tailspin. She couldn't fathom telling her father she was married.

"No. Definitely not," she said quickly. "We'll, uh… we'll move to your place."

"Dr. Stratton?" A nurse popped her head into the makeshift room. "They need you in 2-C."

"Alright, great," he said as he swiftly switched to what she'd figured out was his "doctor voice." Jack stood up and kissed Addy firmly on the lips. "I'll call you when I get off work."

The nurse rolled her eyes good-naturedly.

"Okay," Addy said quietly. "Hey!" she called after him. "Wait! I need your number."

Jack turned around and grinned. "It's already in your phone. Don't you remember?"

"My phone? No …"

"You were quite insistent that you would remember. You put me in as Dr. Hottie."

Addy felt her face flush red. "Oh, God …"

"But I think you changed it on the wedding night. See you later, wifey."

As Jack left, Addy pulled out her phone. There was nothing under Dr. Hottie, but there was a new recent contact. "Husband."

Addy hung her head. *I have no idea what I'm in for.*

5

Jack put Addy's last box in the Jeep. He frowned down at the four boxes, and glanced at the additional two piled in the backseat of her car.

Either she lives a really disgustingly minimalistic life, or she's not planning on keeping this up for long, he thought.

He crossed his arms and gazed up at the front porch of her house. Jack hadn't known what to expect when she gave him the address. He still didn't. She was adamant that he stay outside, and already had the six boxes neatly lined up on the front steps ready to go.

"What if I have to use the toilet?" he'd asked when he arrived and she physically blocked him from the stairs.

"Use the bushes!"

"Why? What are you hiding in there?"

"Nothing," she'd stressed, and pushed one of the boxes into his hands.

From the outside, it looked like a typical, classic Tahoe house. Designed like a large cabin, it had plenty of rustic charm and a porch swing that could use a paint job.

"Big house for just three people," he told her. "It looks like a bed and breakfast."

"It wasn't always just three people," she'd muttered.

He'd backed off then, reminded that her mother was still a sore spot for her.

"What do you mean you're moving? What's gotten into you?" Her bewildered little sister, Kenzie, faced off against Addison on the porch. Kenzie's eyes were wide.

"Who goes off and marries a total stranger? Especially you! You were always the responsible one, the planner. I look away for two seconds at the bar, and you're halfway to Reno with someone who could totally be a serial killer for all we know. No offense," she called down to Jack.

"None taken. I do know how to use a scalpel, after all."

"Don't worry about it, I know what I'm doing," Addy hissed. "Did you get my email? Dad has to have the pills split into morning and evening doses, or they're not effective. And the cleaners always come on the second Tuesday of the month, so don't deadbolt the door on those days. Kenzie, are you listening? The whole house can't fall apart just because—"

"Oh my God, *yes*, I get it, okay? And I got your freaking three-page checklist. Just… go have fun with your hot doctor husband, okay? Go bonk your brains out or whatever." Kenzie gave a sudden laugh. "Maybe we're more alike than I thought."

"I wouldn't take it that far," Addy said, and Kenzie wrapped her arms around her.

"I'll miss you," Kenzie said, barely loud enough for Jack to hear.

"I'll see you almost every day at the restaurant."

"It's not the same."

Jack looked away. That kind of familiar affection made him nervous. It was foreign to him, and he felt like he'd stepped into something he wasn't meant to see.

His family just didn't do affection. He imagined what would happen if he hugged his mother the way that Kenzie has just hugged Addy. *Distressed* would be one way to put it, that was for sure.

He sat in the Jeep to wait out the goodbyes, and couldn't help but think of his own family back in Melbourne. His own parents had never been in the same room as one another if they could help it. And after his dad died, his mother had seemed ... almost relieved. He'd never attributed that word to it before, but that's what it was. Like a weight had been lifted from her life.

"Ready?" Addy was at his window, a cautious smile on her face.

"I am. Are you?"

"I guess so. As ready as I'm going to be. This isn't so strange, right?" she asked as she dropped her voice to a whisper. "I mean, in some countries, people get married and they've never even seen each other before."

"Yeah. But I think a little more thought and preparation goes into arranged marriages compared to what we're doing."

He kept an eye in the rearview mirror as she followed him to his condo.

"This is where you live?" she asked, nervous. "This is where Jeremy lives."

"Oh yeah? I think I've seen him around, now that you mention it. I had a pretty unpleasant run-in with him, and that was without the news of our marriage! Maybe it'll be easier to make him jealous than I thought."

She looked around as he picked up the two boxes from her car. She trailed him to the house.

"Well, this is it!" He pushed open the door with a flourish.

Addy wrinkled her nose and looked around. "Not much for decorating, huh? Or furniture?"

"I figured those could be some of your first wifely duties. Decorating and furniture shopping."

"Ha ha," she said, and took one of the boxes from him. "At least you got a couch. A new one. It still has the tag on it."

"Oh, yeah, sorry 'bout that," he said. "It was just delivered a few days ago. Look around. I'd give you the grand tour, but that seems a bit formal."

He grabbed a beer out of the fridge as he listened to her footsteps down the short hall.

"It's just one bedroom," she said, already done with the tour. She gave him an accusing look and opened her mouth, speech clearly prepared.

"Don't worry, I'll take the couch," he said and held his hand up. "I washed the sheets on the bed and everything. It's all yours, nice and clean."

"Well. Okay," she said.

Side by side, they went out to the cars to grab the next load of boxes, only to see Jeremy's truck. It blocked in both their cars. Jeremy was en route to his own condo, but broke out with a laugh when he saw them.

"What's so funny?" she asked. Jack hadn't heard that kind of edge in her voice before. "Actually, never mind. I'm not surprised that you'd think marriage is a joke."

"Marriage?" Jeremy asked, incredulous. He pulled down his sunglasses. "Yeah, good luck getting anybody to believe that bullshit. What, did the Aussie need a green card or something?"

"You—"

Before she could finish saying anything, Jack grabbed her and dipped her nearly to the ground. His lips met hers and even he was surprised by the magnetic pull between them. She let out a small gasp, and he took the opportunity to slip his tongue between her teeth. For a moment, he forgot where he was—or that it was all a ruse. She knotted her fist in his shirt and pulled him closer, afraid he might drop her, and the cuteness of it made his heart surge.

Finally, he pulled her back up and she let out another gasp for breath. Jeremy was silent before them, and Jack offered up a grin.

"Fuck off," Jeremy said with a scowl. With hunched shoulders, he stalked to his building.

"That was Oscar-worthy acting," Addy whispered to him.

They dumped the rest of the boxes on the counter and Addy headed for the fridge.

"I'm starving," she said. "I was too busy packing this morning to eat. There's nothing in here," she said as she held the door open and looked at him.

"It was a bachelor pad until just now, remember? Don't worry, I'll order a pizza."

"Um, yeah, because I'm not about to make a dinner of beer and... Vegemite? Seriously?"

"Americans have mac and cheese. We have Vegemite. Comfort food, what can I say?"

"Yeah, that's all yours."

"What about the beer? I know that's on your Addison-approved list."

She put her hands on her hips. "I meant real food. Besides, it didn't exactly work out great the last time we had beer together."

"Alright, alright, I'll call the pizza place again."

"Again?"

"Yeah, let's ... let's just say they know me there. I'm already a regular, and I've only been in this country for about a week! That's impressive, right?"

"Not quite the word I'd use. Tomorrow, I'll stop by the store after my shift. Man cannot live on pizza alone."

"The store? So, are you saying ... are you ..."

"Am I what? Capable of grocery shopping?"

"I mean, are you any good at cooking?"

"I'll have you know that I learned from my mother, who used to cook everything at the restaurant before she..." Addison's eyes started to water and her words faded. "Anyway, what do you want? For dinner tomorrow, I mean?"

"Um... how about... cheeseburgers?"

"Yeah, I get enough cheeseburgers at work. Besides, aren't you a doctor? Don't you know they're heart attack bombs? How do you feel about lasagna?"

"Great? I guess? What do you want on the pizza?" He hadn't seen this authoritative side of her, at least not directed at him. And he wasn't sure how he felt about it.

"Anything but pineapple. You know the whole Hawaiian pizza thing was originally designed as a joke?"

Jack dialed the number, the third most recent call in his log. He sipped on a beer while he watched her unpack, but couldn't quite figure out what most of the stuff was. She moved so fast as she zipped between rooms that it made him dizzy.

"Slow down, express train. Pizza's here," he said when he heard the knock at the door.

"Where do we eat?" she asked as she emerged from the bathroom. She'd tied her hair up in a messy knot on top of her head and her cheeks were flushed from the unpacking. Something about it, complete with that little tank top and cut-off jeans, made her look carefree and innocent in a way he hadn't noticed before.

"How about my bed?"

"Excuse me?"

"I meant the couch. You know? My bed?"

"Yeah, you're so funny," she said, but she accepted the plate he handed her and pulled out a generous slice.

"You know?" he asked as they sat side by side and stared out the window. "I've never really lived with a girl before."

"Never really? Or never-never?" she asked.

"Never-never. Maybe I should get to know you a little better to make the experience… not so freaking weird. So you were born here, right?"

"Yep. Don't be jealous."

"Didn't you ever want to get away? I mean, before college?"

"Only every single day of my life. It got worse when my mom was diagnosed… well, let's just say that my wanderlust hasn't died." She grabbed another slice and propped her feet up on the boxes, a makeshift coffee table.

"So, why don't you go?" he asked. "I mean now, especially. What's keeping you here?"

"You've seen my sister," Addy said with a laugh. "Would you leave her in charge of everything? Anything?"

Jack thought about it. "She's not so bad. She's a kid. I mean, think about it. You could be… I dunno, hiking the Himalayas! Something."

Addy shot him a look. "Do you know it costs over sixty thousand to climb Mount Everest? And that's just to try, there's no guarantee you'll make it to the top. You grew up with money, didn't you?"

"I, uh, I guess so. Why?"

"Because sixty thousand is a lot of money. Just walking away from everything to spend weeks 'finding yourself' or whatever costs a lot of money. And if you don't have it... well, you get used to looking at the scenery around you. And you keep your head down. If you're from my family, you thank your lucky stars that you made it to twenty-three. I knew, growing up, that life was a precious commodity—"

"I didn't mean to imply otherwise. Let's change the subject. Tell me something you like."

"Something I like?"

"Yeah, anything."

"Strawberry ice cream."

"Quite the discerning palate. But I agree."

"You tell me something you like."

"Base jumping and deep-sea diving."

"Very frugal choices."

"Hey, I don't judge you, you don't judge me. Your turn."

"Photography," she said, without pause.

"Looking at photographs or taking them?"

"Both. Your turn."

"Race cars."

"Watching them, or owning them and racing them?"

"Both," he said a bit sheepishly. "Your turn. One more."

"Art," she said, and gazed into the distance.

"That doesn't count. Photography is art."

"I'm glad you think so," she said with a small smile.

"You should really go to Rome and Paris. And Barcelona! And Medellín, the Botero statues around the city are amazing—"

"Your privilege is showing," she said with a twinkle in her eye.

"Maybe we'll go there together."

Addy sat up, stiff. "Let's not ... like, make plans and stuff. This isn't real, remember?"

"What? If we're faking a marriage, we can fake a honeymoon? It's no big deal. I'd go anyway, and I'd enjoy the company—"

Addy stood up and picked up the discarded napkins and dirty plates.

"I'll take those," he said. Jack grabbed the plates and dumped them in the trash.

"What are you doing!?"

"We'll buy new ones," he said with a shrug.

"That's wasteful. And arrogant," she said with a scowl.

"Sorry. So, what do you want to do? I can stream Netflix on—"

"Actually, I'm tired. I think I'll just go to bed."

"Bed? But it's just ten o'clock!"

"Some of us have the opening shift."

She disappeared into the bedroom with a solid click of the door.

Damn. Are all women this touchy?

6

Addy groaned as she kicked off her scuffed black Dansko clogs in the small employees' room tucked behind the kitchen. Even the slow season in Tahoe tested her with each shift.

For the past eight hours she'd been on her feet as she rushed from table to table or expertly folded cloth napkins around flatware.

She pulled the tips out of her pockets and apron. Addy had been scheduled for the past ten days straight, not counting the day she'd called off with the hangover to end all hangovers.

Thank God the two new girls I hired will be starting soon, she thought.

"Hey!" Her sister stood in the doorway, fresh-faced and ready to take over the transition from lunch shift to happy hour. "Have you seen Dawn?"

"Yeah," Addy said with a sigh. "I think she went on a dumpster run a few minutes ago. Wasn't that supposed to be your job, Kenzie?"

Her sister wrinkled her nose.

"Sorry, I was running late," she said. "I had to stop for coffee, you know. Can't exactly work the night shift uncaffeinated."

Kenzie held up her staple six-dollar coffee.

"We have coffee here, you know. For free. Have you counted the tills again? Make sure all the menus are switched to dinner, too. And don't forget about the—"

MacKenzie rolled her eyes and turned away.

"Yeah, I'll get to it! Geez, just go home already. All these morning shifts are making you cranky."

"Kenzie!" Addy called to her sister's retreating back.

She jumped up to go after her and heard the clang of change fall to the floor.

"Damn," she whispered under her breath, but shoved her aching feet back into the shoes. She called out again as she bolted down the hall to catch her sister. "Kenzie!"

"What?" Kenzie asked, annoyed. "It's just a restaurant. It's not like it's brain surgery or something."

"You know why this is so important! And it's not 'just' a restaurant. It's Dad's restaurant. Mom and Dad's restaurant..."

Kenzie sighed and put down the coffee.

"I know that," she said slowly. "You think I forgot? And it's not like it's the first time you've reminded me."

Addy crossed her arms.

"Do I think you forgot? Maybe. You forgot three times last week about some pretty basic opening and transition tasks. Luckily for you it *isn't* brain surgery."

"Addison Marie Fuller," Kenzie said as she cocked her head sideways. "Are you saying you don't think I'm smart enough to be a brain surgeon?"

"I just don't know why you have to make everything a struggle for me," Addy grumbled.

Kenzie leaned forward and kissed her on the cheek, just like their mom used to do.

"You worry too much," Kenzie said. "It's not good for you. Premature wrinkles."

She flashed Addy that golden smile that worked on everyone else before she shot out the saloon doors toward the front of the house.

"You forgot to count the tills again," Addy said quietly.

They were still stacked neatly with Addy's precise handwriting on the point of sale tape rolls. She drew in a deep breath and began counting them again herself.

There's no way Dawn can do it, she thought.

Addy and Kenzie had learned quickly that while Dawn could charm her way into making the most tips out of any of them, she was useless when it came to math.

"Oh my God! Addy! Hey!" Kenzie stuck her head into the back.

"What is it now?" Addy asked. "Seriously, I'm not going to help you with—"

"Shh!" Kenzie said in a stage whisper. "Jeremy just came in."

"Jeremy?"

"Don't look," Kenzie said.

"Don't look? Why would you come back here to tell me he's here if you don't want me to look!"

"I just wanted to let you know. In case, you know, you wanted to go out the back…"

"Why would I sneak out the back like *I'm* the one who did something wrong?" Addy asked.

She was suddenly aware that she must look like hell and smell like a fryer. She hated herself for it, but she instinctually reached up to gauge how messy her ponytail was.

"Well…" Kenzie shifted from side to side and glanced over her shoulder.

"Kenzie, what is it? Do I really look that bad?"

"It's just that, you know, he's not alone."

Addy looked at her sister, scrunching her face up. "What do you mean?"

"He's got someone with him," Kenzie said to the floor.

"You must mean Shannon." She reached for a stack of cups that were put away haphazardly, and righted them. "I know about them already."

"I'm sorry." Kenzie said. "I shouldn't have said anything. It's just that I saw him—with her—and I didn't want you to—"

"It's okay, it's not your fault," Addy said. "Coming in here like this, with her…"

"What a dick move," Kenzie said. The little sister in her came out strong, ready to go to battle for Addison. "He's an asshole."

"Yeah, well. She's not much better," Addy said.

It had been five years since she'd graduated high school, but seeing Shannon in person after all those years instantly took her back to being eighteen. She'd had classes with Shannon since they were in sixth grade.

They'd never been friends, but sometime around their junior year of high school Shannon had decided Addy was a target. She could still remember the taunts that trailed after her down the hallways.

"He looks bad," Kenzie said. "I think he's going prematurely bald."

"His hair's buzzed, Kenzie," Addy said.

She hated herself instantly for sticking up for him. Especially after how they'd broken up.

They'd dated for a year, and for the past couple of months Addy had thought they'd simply transitioned to the more complacent stage of their relationship.

The honeymoon stage hadn't been the kind of fireworks she'd always heard about, but Jeremy had been two years ahead of both her and Shannon in high school.

Quarterback of the football team, he'd been his class' homecoming king every year and of course prom king by the time he was a senior. She still remembered the surprising weight of the crown when he'd let her try it on six months ago.

Now, Jeremy was climbing the ranks as a salesman at one of the highest-end jewelry stores in town. Unfortunately, that meant that he had less and less time for her. When she'd eventually worked up the courage to confront him about his neglect of her, he just shrugged.

"So what, you want to break up?" he said.

Like it meant nothing to him. Like *she* meant nothing to him.

She'd left his apartment in tears that night, and it was only a few days later that she had first spotted him slinking around with Shannon. He probably didn't even pick Shannon to bother Addy, he just didn't care about Addy at all.

Kenzie elbowed her in the ribs.

"I'm gonna go kick them out," she said. "I can't believe he had the nerve to come in here—"

Addy grabbed her arm.

"No, let them stay," she said.

Kenzie searched her eyes.

"Fine," she said finally. "But I'm not waiting on them."

Side by side, they peered across the doors. Shannon let out a laugh, and her long platinum hair fell down her back. Addy sighed.

Jeremy had always been the cool guy in high school, somehow able to strike that balance between bad boy and popular guy. Even now, he was still really handsome. The buzzed dirty blond hair highlighted his sharp features and square jawline.

But Kenzie is right, she thought to herself. *His hair is starting to thin. That's really why he buzzes it.*

She shook her head and forced the mean side of her away. There was no denying that she was still in love with him.

Let's be honest, she told herself. *Jeremy barely paid you any attention the past few years. Maybe I am kind of pathetic, but how did I know any different? He was the first cool guy I'd ever dated.*

The others, not that there had been a lot, were nonthreatening and good guys, but there was no fire.

Not that you can expect much from someone who works in a video game store, she thought. *Or an entry-level software developer.*

With Kenzie pressed against her side, they watched Dawn sashay through the dining room and troll for tips. Dawn was thirty-five and married, complete with an oversized rock on her finger, but that didn't stop her flirtations. She let out a whistle worthy of a construction worker when two young guys came in and walked up to the bar.

Addy pulled off her apron and started back down the hallway. She grabbed the restaurant's books to take home.

It's about time to get a handle on them, she thought. *And no way in hell I'm going out the back like some kind of criminal.*

She started to make a mental to-do list as she pushed through the saloon doors and wove through the dining room.

Compare price sheets requested from the vendors. Make next week's schedule. Compose that reply to OSHA's letter.

"Addison! I'm glad to have caught you." Addy turned around, her arms full. Shannon walked toward her.

"You are? Can I... can I help you with something?"

She could have kicked herself for asking, but they were still on restaurant property. She was still basically the acting manager.

"I just wanted to thank you."

"Thank me?"

"Well, yeah." Shannon pushed a lock of hair behind her ear. "Jeremy and I, we're really happy. And I have you to thank for that."

"Me? What did I do?"

"He told me everything. About, you know, your relationship," she said, and dropped her voice low. "He's a good guy, and I know he was trying to do you a favor dating you. Giving you an ego boost and all that."

"Excuse me?"

"Oh, don't take it like that. But thank you for not begging him to stay with you a little longer. You know he would have. That was really big of you, to be all adult about things. I mean, we both know he deserved better. And I'm just glad I was there when he was ready to stop being so charitable."

"Get out of my restaurant," Addy said. Her voice shook and tears stung at her eyes, but she refused to let them fall.

"What? Hey, I'm being nice here!"

"Get the fuck out of my restaurant!" Addy yelled. The silence around them was palpable. She could feel all the eyes in the restaurant on her. She heard a utensil fall to the floor.

"Pathetic," Shannon said with a smile.

Addy turned around, covered in shame, and ran to the front door with the heavy books in her arms.

"Hey! You okay?" She nearly slammed into Jack as she barreled through the front doors.

"No," she whimpered. "I just… can you please take me somewhere else?"

"Of course," he said. "Come on. My car is right over here."

She followed him to his car, still ashamed.

7
───

Jack slid his gaze over to Addy. He was concerned about her. She seemed oblivious to his gaze though, leaning on the window to press her face against the glass. Her face was tear-stained, although she had stopped crying.

"Hey," he said. "Where is the biggest, messiest sandwich in town?"

"Hmm? Oh. I don't know. Maybe Boudreaux's? The have New Orleans-style poboys."

She sniffed, still moody. At least she'd answered his question. He wanted to ask what she was so upset about, but he held his tongue. Maybe later, when she had calmed down.

"Where do I go?" he asked.

"It's on Main Street, next to the post office," she murmured. She went back to looking out the window.

He drove to the restaurant, parking nearby. Boudreaux's proved to be a tiny hole in the wall, all done in rough pine wood. Addy followed him in, obviously still wrapped up in her own thoughts.

It was a order at the front kind of place, so he looked at the menu hanging over the register. After a minute, he ordered a roast beef poboy and some fries. With some encouragement, she ordered a corneal-dusted oyster poboy.

Jack led the way to a table, and they settled in. She didn't seem to be in the mood for talking, so he busied himself by tearing some paper towels off the roll sitting on the table and folding them into cranes.

"A bird?" she asked curiously when he placed the first one before her.

"A crane," he said, sticking his tongue out as he tried to execute a particularly neat fold.

"Where did you learn origami?"

He peeked at her, and saw that she was watching him avidly, eyes curious. He suppressed a smile. He'd used origami to impress women before, but never to charm them out of a bad mood.

"My father taught me," he said. "He was a surgeon, so he studied origami as a way to hone his physical dexterity. He always had some kind of paper creation in his pockets."

"That sounds fun."

"It was. He would come home from a long shift at the hospital, and empty his pockets. He'd have folded cranes and frogs and flowers, and I would play with them. It's one of the things I missed most after he died."

She bit her lip, but the look of curiosity was still clear on her face. A server brought over their food, and they were quiet for a minute while they tasted everything. Addy snagged one of Jack's fries, offering a quick smile when he raised a brow.

He took a big bite of his sandwich, managing to get roast beef and lettuce everywhere. Addy laughed, and tore off another paper towel to offer him.

"Thanks," he said, wiping his mouth. "You weren't kidding about the level of messiness. God, this is good though."

"I never joke about food." She punctuated her remark by taking a huge bite of her sandwich, and sighing with pleasure as she chewed. "They really know how to make a sandwich here."

"There's something about watching a hot woman manhandle a sandwich the size of her head..." he teased.

"You're just jealous that you didn't get the oysters." She smirked.

"So you want to know about my father's death, right?" he ventured.

She made a considering face, and nodded. "I don't want to bum you out. But yeah, I do."

"I'll make you a deal. I'll tell you about him, if you will tell me why you left your restaurant crying earlier."

She pulled a face but nodded. "That's fair."

"Okay," he said, after taking another bite. "So my dad died of Huntington's disease when I was thirteen."

Her eyes widened. "Really?"

"Yup. My parents were already married when they found out that my father had it. It's inherited, obviously. From what I gather, my paternal grandfather probably had it too, but he died in a car accident when my father was a baby."

She pushed the remnants of her sandwich away.

"If you don't mind me asking, have you been tested to see if you're a carrier?"

"I got tested when I turned eighteen," he said, toying with one of the paper towel cranes. "It was negative. Mum made me. If it were up to me, I wouldn't have been tested."

"Why not?" she asked.

"I don't know," Jack said truthfully. "What's the point? It's not like anything could be done if I did have the gene. I probably shouldn't say this, as a medical professional, but I think some things are just destined. What difference would it make if I knew I had the gene for Huntington's or not?"

"I guess that's true," she said as she nodded slowly. "But still, there are experimental procedures. More time to consider naturopathic or alternative therapies in conjunction with Western medicine's best practices. If it were me—"

"But it's not," he said simply. He smiled at Addy to let her know he wasn't judging.

"No. I suppose it isn't."

"Are you satisfied now?"

She scrunched up her face, making him chuckle.

"Let me know if it's prying, seriously," she said, shaking her finger at him. "Is your father the reason you got into medicine?"

"Yeah," Jack said. "I guess it is. I mean, he was a surgeon for years, and then he was treated by so many doctors... I guess I was around hospitals for all my formative years."

He'd always known that, but had never said it aloud before.

"That's not uncommon," Addy said. "I've heard of a lot of doctors who spent an inordinate amount of time in hospitals as children. Either because of an illness themselves, or a family member."

"Mmm," Jack said noncommittally. "All right. Enough about me. Tell me about what made you cry at the restaurant."

"Oh," she said, turning pink. "It seems silly, after... all that."

"And yet, it's what I want to know. We made a deal, remember?"

"Well, you put it in perspective, to say the least. But... well, you know my ex?"

"Yeah. Jeremy. He's a piece of work."

"Well, he came in with his new girlfriend."

"Into your restaurant?"

"Yep. Shannon. She's a girl I went to high school with, and she hasn't changed a bit since. She's still blonde, pretty, and *mean*."

"Did you kick them out?" he asked. The waiter came and took their plates away, and Jack was quick to drop to twenties on the table.

"Well... I did say, 'get the F out of my restaurant'. But only after she said some really atrocious stuff to me. And then I cried, and I ran outside. That's when you found me."

"Jeez. Well, did you at least embarrass her in the bargain?"

"I mean, I made a scene. Everyone in the restaurant turned and looked."

"Good girl," he said, leaning back in his seat. "Also, what a dick! To bring his new chick to your restaurant..."

"The whole thing was ridiculous."

"Not to change the subject, but... do you feel like ice cream? I think there's a place just a couple doors down."

She laughed, shaking her head. "Ice cream, after a poboy sandwich? Now that is decadent."

"I'll have you know, I treat *all* my wives this well. Especially the hot ones," he said, winking at her. She flushed. The color looked good on her, the light pink bringing out the blue in her eyes.

"All right, well since you treat all your wives this way…"

He stood up and offered her his arm, and she rose and took it. Her touch was light, but he still felt a bit charged by it, like she was made of pure energy.

As they strolled down the block, he looked down on her. She was tall enough for a woman, but at 6'2 he dwarfed her nonetheless.

He could easily imagine them in bed together, her curled up at his side, reading a book. She would fit against him nicely, his tanned complexion standing out against her flawless pale one.

Then he made the mistake of thinking about why they would be in bed together. He could just imagine her riding his cock, her head tossed back and her mouth open. God, the things he could do to that sweet mouth…

"Wait," she said, tugging on his arm. "This is Fifty Licks."

"Oh," he said.

Damn, even the way she says the name of the ice cream parlor is sexy.

She pushed open the door, releasing his arm. He followed her inside, unsettled. He wasn't sure why he was having these fantasies about her.

Not that she wasn't beautiful. She was, truly.

She just wasn't his type. All of his exes looked like Rosalie; they were tall, thin, and willowy. Usually blonde, with a competitive personality. The problem was, he'd had Rosalie. She was the dream, right?

But he hadn't ended up with her. If he remembered correctly, he'd dumped Rosalie pretty spectacularly.

He looked at Addy, who was bent over at the display case, examining the flavors. She was so petite, and lacking in the long-limbed grace that all his exes had in spades. There was something about her, though.

Something unique. She turned to him, her huge smile

infectious. She was enthusiastic about a flavor, beckoning to him to come try it.

He walked over as she got two samples from the girl behind the counter. She offered one of the pink spoons with a little chocolate blob of ice cream to him, and he took it.

"Omigod," she said, her eyes fluttering shut. She took a second taste, savoring it. "This is soooo good."

It was good, but watching her enjoy it was better.

"We'll have two of these," he said to the girl behind the counter. "In waffle cones."

Addy finished the sample and eyed him with amusement. "That's the first one we tasted!"

"I know what I like," he said with a shrug. "It's that simple."

"I wish I was more like that," she said as he paid for their ice cream. "I'm always concerned that I'm missing something really great because of something that's only *good*."

"FOMO?" he asked.

"Huh?"

"Fear of missing out. That's the name for what you just described."

"Ah. Well, I guess that's it."

She led the way out of the shop, where they found a spot at one of the tables. He watched her as she licked the sides of her ice cream, careful not to let it drip. He watched her pink tongue dark out and retreat over and over again.

He shook his head at himself, and refocused on his own ice cream cone. If he wasn't careful, he was going to end up fantasizing about all the other things she could do with that little mouth of hers...

And that wasn't the point of their outing today. Hell, it wasn't really the point of anything between them, though he was starting to wonder about that.

What was the point of their... relationship? He could shove almost anyone under his mum's nose. Why Addy?

He looked up at her and she gave him a lopsided grin. He chuckled.

He told himself that he didn't need a reason. He could've woken up next to almost anyone in Reno. It wasn't about her.
...right?

8

She could tell even as she opened her eyes at dawn that Jack wasn't in the condo. He had a presence when he was there, regardless of what room he was in, constantly moving.

Addy stretched out in the bed and pressed deeper into the new, firm mattress. They'd lived together for just five days, and had hardly seen each other in that time. Not that she could complain.

Addy had been quick to sign on for double shifts at the restaurant. She'd trained the new hires herself, and Kenzie was happy to skip out on that aspect of the job.

Jack's hours at the hospital had quickly increased as the town accepted the medical center as more convenient than the other options—and it didn't hurt that the new doctors in town looked like they did.

Occasionally, they'd pass each other in the hallway or bump into one another in the kitchen. Those encounters usually entailed a few polite hellos and nothing more. A few times, Addy had been rushing out the door just as Jack arrived home from an eighteen-hour shift at the hospital.

Is this really what married life is like? she wondered. If so, it didn't seem like she was missing out on much.

Even stretched out, she could tell her feet ached from so

many hours at the restaurant. Her right forearm was tired from carrying heavy trays.

Addy reached for the sketchbook she kept beside the bed and flipped to a blank page. With a hard charcoal pencil, she started to sketch the first thing that came to mind. A slice of cherry pie that she'd dropped in the middle of the dining room yesterday.

It had splattered like blood across her white apron and the just-scrubbed floors. Someone at the bar had given her a slow clap.

"Can't you think about anything besides work?" she asked herself as she filled in the details.

The big pieces of chunky sugar that topped it. The way the baker had tightly folded the crust edge. She hated herself for not being able to turn off work mode, but she finished the sketch.

Complete, she snapped the book shut and pulled herself out of bed. Finally, she'd be able to fully stock the kitchen like she'd promised Jack. What better use of a day off than to trudge through household chores?

Plus, the bathroom lacked everything but a shower liner.

Might as well take care of that, too.

Addy stretched her arms overhead as she walked to the kitchen. She closed her eyes and enjoyed the cool air against her bare midriff as her t-shirt crept up her abdomen. Her eyes snapped open as the side door to the kitchen burst open.

"'Bout time, lazybones," Jack said. He cradled two coffees from the good drive-thru in his hands.

"Jesus! Jack, I thought you were working today."

"I was, I just got off. Coffee?"

"Aren't you... aren't you tired?"

"Tired? But it's morning."

"Yeah, but not for you."

"Do you want the coffee or not?"

She bit her lip and looked at the two large white paper cups. "What kind is it?"

"Dunno. Americano, I think."

"Black?"

"What, is my wife racist?"

"I meant... never mind. I like it with a lot of cream and Splenda. Which I'm guessing you don't have."

"You guessed right. But I do have sugar and skim milk."

Addy wrinkled her nose, but took the nearly-empty carton of milk when he handed it to her.

"This expires today," she said.

"Good thing you're going to use it, then." Jack shoved the white and pink bag of sugar with a spoon stuck in it toward her.

Addy added what she thought was the smallest amount possible to make the coffee bearable.

"So! Your day off, right? What's the plan? What do you want to do?"

She looked up at Jack through her thick lashes. *God, he was really raring to go.*

"Well, I was going to get the groceries. And the bathroom really needs—"

"I was thinking gliding," he interrupted.

He'd taken the lid off his own coffee and generously sucked down the steaming liquid.

"Gliding," she repeated.

"Sure! It's a great opportunity here, I've looked into it. And we'll get a great view of Reno," he said with a wink.

"Jack, I don't really have time for—"

"C'mon, we're newlyweds, aren't we? Shouldn't we be putting tons of pictures on Facebook or something? Polluting all our social media channels with happy photos?"

She paused. He had her, there.

What was the point of this whole sham if they weren't going to really sell it? Who would be jealous of them if all they did was disappear into their jobs?

"Well, I guess. God, how do you have so much energy? When's the last time you slept?"

He grinned at her but stayed silent. That look made her heart start to beat faster.

"Well?" she asked to fill the silence.

"I just slept seven straight hours in the break room at the hospital. Totally recharged my batteries."

"You *slept* there? You didn't have night rotations? Why didn't you come home?" It felt alien to say home, but Addy didn't know how to take it back.

"You miss me?" he asked with a wink.

"No! I just meant—"

"Addy. I know it's weird to have me sleeping in here. I finished my rotation, it was the middle of the night, and I knew I'd probably wake you up if I came home. There was a bed right there. It's not like the couch here is the king of comfort, you know."

"Sorry," she said, and lowered her eyes.

"Don't be. So? Gliding?"

"Let me get my camera."

Addy threw on a pair of jeans, grabbed her purse and DSLR, and shoved her sunglasses on as she swept her hair into a messy ponytail.

Jack held the door of his Jeep open for her—the passenger side was the only part of the car that had some semblance of a door, though it was just a frame.

"Oh, so is this like a real date?" she teased.

He just shrugged and jumped into his side. As they merged onto the highway, the wind and sounds of Tahoe raged against her.

Of all the cars to pick, he had to go with an open Jeep with no top or sides. But she had to admit it fit him. *He looks so comfortable like this, wind in his hair, a man in control of his surroundings.*

"Care for a detour?" he called to her over the wind.

"What do you have in mind?"

"Maybe a drive by Jeremy's father's current construction project? He's working on it, right?"

"Yeah, how—how do you know that?"

"Not hard to find things out in a small town," he said, and smiled over at her.

As they approached the site, flaggers pumped their hands at Jack and gestured at him to slow down. Addy spotted Jeremy's truck immediately, the biggest one on site.

As they crawled by, she saw Jeremy's broad back. He wore that Metallica t-shirt she'd always hated.

Jeremy felt their eyes on him and turned slowly. The hard hat he wore cast a mean shadow across his face. Addy grinned over at Jack.

"I think it worked," she said.

"Of course it did, love."

Jack maneuvered the Jeep up a dirty trail she'd never noticed before. As they climbed to a high point, she saw an unfamiliar Jeep, one with actual doors, and a man with what looked like a strange, supersized paper plane on the cliff.

"What is this, Jack?" she asked nervously. "I thought we were going hang gliding."

"I never said hang. I said gliding. Like a sailplane."

"A *plane?*"

Jack grabbed a small backpack out of the backseat and jumped out. "Coming?" he asked.

She scrambled after him and caught up just as he slapped the glider professional on the back. "Is this, like, skydiving?" she asked. "Like tandem, or whatever it's called? Are you taking us up?" she asked the man in the official jacket with the "Sail Away" logo.

"Me?" the guide asked. He looked vaguely familiar. Addy was sure they'd probably gone to school together. "I mean, I can. But Jack said—"

"I'm an experienced pilot," Jack told her. "Done this tons of times, don't worry."

"Don't worry?" she repeated, incredulous.

"Okay, now, since Jack is licensed and he's piloting, I just need to go over the basic safety procedures for you, Addy."

The guide began to tick off his prepared speech, but her heart hammered so heavily in her head she couldn't digest anything he said. Instead, she took in the glider, aware of how flimsy it looked.

The actual plane part was tiny, and the wings and tail stretched out long and slender. It was like a pretty supermodel version of a plane.

"Got it?"

"Sorry, what?" she asked sheepishly and looked at the guide.

"Just sign the waiver, here, in all the blank boxes."

She looked to Jack.

"Go ahead," he said. "Trust me."

Addy didn't know what made her do it, but she watched her hand take the pen and signed her life away. She couldn't have stopped it if she wanted to. And she wasn't sure what she wanted anymore.

"These look like paper planes gone wrong," she said as Jack grabbed her hand and led her to the cockpit.

He laughed, but when she saw how close they had to sit together, her fear began to transition to excitement.

If he's an experienced pilot, you're safe. Right?

As they climbed in, she quickly reached for the seatbelt while Jack gave the guide a thumbs up. Addy pulled the camera strap over her neck.

"Ready?" Jack asked. Addy shook her head no, but Jack started the winch and almost immediately they were off the ground.

"Oh my God," she said as she watched the ground disappear below them. "This thing goes fast."

She gripped the edge of her seat.

Jack laughed. "Relax!"

"That's easy for you to say."

Still, after a couple of minutes, it was clear that he really did know what he was doing. The way he expertly guided the glider put her at ease—or as much as could be expected.

"Wow. It really is beautiful," she said under her breath. She'd never seen her small town like this before. Slowly, Addy lifted her camera and began to take photos.

"You know, the first time I was in a glider? I was just a kid. My dad took me up. Been addicted ever since," Jack said. "I even thought about being a pilot."

"I thought you were," she said, and shot him a look.

"You know what I mean. A commercial pilot."

"So why didn't you?"

"Eh, you know how it is. Lawyer or doctor, those were the only two possible professions approved by the family. Doctor seemed a little more exciting than lawyer."

"High standards in your family. I'm sure your wife the waitress will fit right in," she said. Addy meant it as a joke, but knew it didn't sound that way.

Maybe because you aren't really joking.

"I didn't mean it like that," Jack said quickly. "I mean, those standards are just for me—"

"You know, I like this a lot more than flying in real planes," she said, eager to change the subject.

Inside, though, she thought: *what do you mean those standards are just for you?*

"Yeah?"

"I've only flown a handful of times, though. Mostly just to Arizona or New Mexico for college. And I had to take Xanax just to make it seem okay."

"You did? Sorry, I didn't know. You seem okay right now, though."

"Yeah," she agreed. "Maybe it's more the airport and all the rules you have to follow …"

"We'll need to get you a passport."

"Sorry? Is there… something planned?"

"No, not at the moment. But planning isn't my thing. You should always have a passport with plenty of pages waiting to go though."

"Oh, well. Okay. Kenzie has one."

"Yeah? She travel a lot?"

Addy laughed. "Hardly. One road trip to Tijuana for spring break and the car broke down halfway to California."

"Bummer. I'm guessing you've never been removed from a flight, then?" he asked. "Given your limited flight experience and all."

"Uh, no. Definitely not. I bet you have, though."

"You would win with that bet," he said.

Addy was silent as she mulled everything over. *How did I end up here, looking down on my little town with some crazy wealthy doctor adrenaline junkie?*

"Did we mess up our lives?" she finally asked. "Not getting the annulment right away?"

"Well... I'm having a good time. Aren't you?"

"Sure," she said. "I mean ... how can I complain?"

"I think we're alright, then. Oh, look! A river."

"No, that's Martis Creek Lake," she said.

Addy spent the rest of the flight pointing out landmarks she knew, and steered clear of any serious talk.

It's better this way, she thought. *Light and easy. I mean, it's just a couple of months, right?*

"Time to head back," Jack said as he glanced at his watch.

"Already?" she asked.

He laughed. "You want more?"

"It just went so fast."

As they started to descend, she felt the panic set in that she'd felt before at airports. Jack grabbed her hand reassuringly. Addy held her breath as the ground got closer and let it out in a gust of relief as they touched down.

Jack jumped out and leaned down to help her out.

"Okay?" he asked.

She was aware of how closely they were pressed against one another. As she nodded and gazed up, she thought there was a flicker of interest in his eyes. Jack looked down to her lips, and she licked them out of instinct.

"Smile," he said, and whipped out his phone.

He held it above them and kissed her on the cheek for the selfie. Addy felt her face flush.

I'm not disappointed, she told herself. *This is all just to show Jeremy that he messed up, anyway.*

It would just be a lot easier if Jack wasn't so damn handsome.

9
─────

He was disappointed when he pulled up to the condo and Addy's car wasn't there.

Why? he wondered to himself. *You miss her or something?*

It was strange. They'd only been in this faux marriage for two weeks and he'd somehow settled into a kind of routine. It felt almost… normal.

Jack opened the front door and realized that slowly, Addy had started to become more prominent in their shared space. Little pieces of her had started to appear.

A framed photo of her and her college roommate on the bookshelf. Her favorite lavender scarf hung on the hook by the door.

He opened up his laptop and saw thirty-nine new notifications on the Facebook tab. It was working. Daily, he'd cultivated a few new photos that highlighted the ideal newlywed relationship.

From Instagram to Tumblr, he'd expertly taken to building a fake, but beautiful life with his new bride.

Whether it was a photo of an amazing view he tagged her in, or simply a photo of her that was snapped on the patio on one of the rare moments they were home together, Jack had to admit that he was pretty good at this. Anyone would think they were in idyllic newlywed bliss.

Jack clicked on the notifications just to clear them. There were comments of congratulations from both of their friends. Some of his he hadn't spoken to in years.

He thumbed through his phone to upload the selection of the day. As he swiped through the photos, filtering some and deleting others, he stopped short at the last photo he'd taken when they'd gone gliding.

Addy was freshly flushed, cheeks a warm pink as he kissed her. He looked closely at the photo—at her. Everything had happened so fast, the night at Dusty's.

The rush into marriage, the moving in together, he'd never really *looked* at her before.

Of course, he knew she was hot. He couldn't help but notice those sunkissed legs as she ran around the house in cut-off shorts. He'd caught his breath a couple of times on the rare occasions she let her hair down. It was so long that it licked the small of her back.

But those were cursory things about her. Easy and obvious. In the photo, he could see the real her. The Addy that he'd grown so accustomed to so fast.

Actually, you don't know her at all, he reminded himself.

He drank in the unnerving blue of her eyes. There were depths there, flecks of gold and green. It was so intense, it was like she cradled galaxies in her eyes.

Her skin was soft, supple, and that kind of all-American golden bronzed that only came from a lifetime of growing up near a lake. A spray of freckles burst across her cheeks and nose, concentrated most along the bridge.

Her eyelashes were unnaturally black, lush and thick. Her lips crested with a sharp cupid's bow that lent a kind of permanent pout.

Faintly, just between her thick and shapely brows, he could make out the light worry marks bred from years of woes he knew almost nothing about.

It made her look wise, like she'd lived. That small so-called flaw was what made her so perfect.

But it wasn't just her face. He remembered the curves of her body as he'd pulled her out of the cockpit. How he could feel the hourglass figure beneath her loose t-shirt.

The way her hips spanned out, a perfect surprise of a curve above her lean body, toned by hard work and not hours grueling away at the gym.

He shook his head.

How could he have never realized before how beautiful she was? Not just sexy, not cute, but truly beautiful.

Jack hated to admit it, but when they'd first met, all he'd really seen when he looked at her was that she wasn't like the other girls he'd dated. And that had been enough for him.

She wasn't blonde, she wasn't tall, and she wasn't insanely thin from constantly working out.

When he'd met Rosalie for instance, he was struck by her magnitude. She was achingly thin, but with her height and her haughty confidence she'd made it seem like it was natural. Like every man should want her, and he'd fallen for it.

However, the first time he'd pulled Rosalie close, he'd almost pulled back in shock at how thin she was. But he'd trudged forward because every other guy in their program had wanted her so badly.

Now, as he looked at Addison, as he really saw her for the first time, he realized how hot she was.

Ridiculously smoking hot, he corrected himself. How had he never seen it before? Why weren't all the guys in this podunk town knocking down her door? *Maybe they were, and you were just so caught up in your own interests you didn't realize.*

Mentally, he patted himself on the back.

You made a good choice, mate, even if you were totally blotto at the time. He racked his brain for clues that she might have dropped. *Was she a hot commodity around here?*

He didn't know—and part of him was ashamed for going back to his old habits of basing someone's worth on what everyone around him thought.

"Hey," Addy's voice broke through his thoughts. Embarrassed, Jack shut off his phone and snapped the laptop shut.

"Hey. Long day?" he asked.

She groaned and slumped onto the couch next to him.

"The longest," she said. "And not just that, the worst."

"What happened?"

Exhaustion emanated from her. She smelled of fresh baked pies and real vanilla.

"Well, for starters, the deep freezer and dishwasher stopped working at the same time. It's like they were in on it together, total nightmare. The repair guy is there now. I just couldn't wait around for him to tell me the bad news."

"Bad news?"

"Yeah. I've suspected for a while now that the dishwasher is on its last leg. It probably has to be replaced. And the deep freezer, it's a miracle it's lasted as long as it has. It's ancient, rusty —I think it's the same one that my... well, never mind."

"Dishwashers and freezers aren't that expensive, are they?" Jack asked. "I mean, I don't know American prices, but—"

"These aren't, like, the dishwashers you buy for homes. They're commercial kitchen grade."

"So, what, like... ten grand?"

"Probably fifteen."

"Oh. Well, I can lend it to you."

"Sorry?" Addy rolled her head to the side and looked at him.

"It's no problem, just fifteen thousand—"

"That's a... nice offer. But I can't take your money."

"Seriously, Addy, you're my wife, remember? No big deal. Besides, I know where you sleep. Right over there!"

"I'm serious too, Jack. I'll figure something else out. Right now, I just need to relax for a minute."

"No, I know what you need."

Addy visibly stiffened. "You... you do?"

"Yeah. Hold on," Jack pushed himself up and sauntered into the kitchen.

He pulled the bottle of whiskey he'd picked up the day he landed in Tahoe out of the corner cupboard along with two cut crystal tumblers.

"Fancy," Addy said. She leaned around the couch and watched him. "How long have you been hiding that in there?"

"Wouldn't you like to know. Rocks or neat?"

"Rocks."

He put three cubes in each of the glasses and filled them one-quarter of the way. With a flourish, he handed Addy her glass and set the bottle down on the little side table she'd picked up last week.

"Jack Daniels," she said. "Cute. Is that the only hard alcohol you drink?"

"Like I've never heard that before. Cheers," he said.

They clinked glasses and he watched her wince at the burn. "Is this your answer for everything?" she asked.

"Pretty much, yes. It works, doesn't it?"

They finished the first few pulls quickly, and Addy refilled their glasses. He let the sweet burn coat his throat as they settled into the depths of the couch.

Jack could see her loosen up. When she got slightly tipsy, just like that first night, the constant air of worry that clouded over her dissipated.

Addy let out a sharp, sudden laugh.

"What's so funny?" he asked, faintly aware that he'd started to slur.

"Nothing. I was just remembering. Well... I had a dream. About you." She buried her face in her forearm and the ice cubes tinkled in the glass. "Forget it, it's too embarrassing, even buzzed."

"About me?" Jack leaned forward. "Like a ... like a sex dream?"

"What? No! God, no. We weren't... we didn't... do anything."

"Oh," he leaned back, disappointed. "Well, way to build up the hype and then smash it back down."

"Just because it didn't have to do with sex doesn't mean—"

"Has anyone ever told you you're really repressed?"

She turned red. "What, are you a psychiatrist now as well as an MD?"

"Psychiatrists are MDs, actually."

"Whatever. You were just in the dream, that's all. We were at the hospital. And Rosalie came by, and you wouldn't kiss me. You said I was a bad kisser."

"Are you?"

"No! Well... I hope not. I don't know, you've kissed me before. You should know..."

Jack squinted and pretended not to remember. "I'm not sure, I can't remember. It must not have been very memorable."

Addy's mouth dropped open, horrified. *"What?"*

"Maybe we should practice. You know, so that way when we kiss in public, it looks authentic."

Addy set her glass down and sputtered. "Wow, really? I mean... if that's what you think we need to do—"

Jack laughed and slapped her thigh.

"Calm down," he said.

The heat that radiated from her leg sparked against his skin. He pulled her closer, somewhere between comfortably buzzed and more serious than he wanted to be.

Addy's eyes widened. He felt himself grow hard as he leaned in. She closed her eyes when he was inches away. The quaint charm of it was intoxicating.

Her head tilted back, an invitation, and his lips met hers. Jack realized it was the first semisober, real kiss they'd ever shared.

As his tongue flicked against her teeth and explored her mouth, she mewled and her breath grew ragged. The little animal noises had him rock hard.

What would it be like to have her? To let her be on top, taking all the pleasure she wanted?

Jack started to lower her down on the couch, but a shatter stopped them both. Her half-full glass of whiskey had toppled to the floor.

"Sorry," she said meekly.

Jack rose up on his hands, his breath so heavy it filled the room.

Addy wiped at her mouth and stood up, wobbling slightly. Jack felt his heart sink. She was clearly drunk, or nearly there.

"I think maybe you should get a glass of water and go to bed," he said. "Don't worry about the glass, I'll clean it up."

She opened her mouth like she was going to say something, but then changed her mind. She turned and headed toward the bedroom.

He saw her turn and give him one last look before she disappeared and closed the door.

10

She leaned against the doorframe of the restaurant's kitchen as the repairman droned on about all the problems she already suspected. "It would cost more to repair them than it would to buy them new. And I get nothing if you replace them, so that should tell you something."

Addy sighed. "So, what are we talking?"

"I mean, it can vary. Depending on what you want, brand ... but I would estimate maybe twelve thousand altogether. If you do some bargain hunting, you might be able to find some deals. Or if you can wait until Labor Day sales—"

"I can't wait even a day without having a dishwasher and freezer," she said.

"Sorry?"

"No," she said with a shake of her head. "I'm sorry, it's not your fault. Do you have any recommendations for affordable commercial appliances?"

"Sure, sure," he said. With grimy black hands, he pulled a stack of business cards out of his wallet. "This guy's local, he'll treat you right. Tell him I sent you."

"And what do I owe you? For the diagnostics, and everything?"

"I'll send you an invoice tomorrow," he said.

She walked him to the front of the restaurant and chewed on

her lip the entire way. Paying for the new appliances would completely drain her personal savings. Addy couldn't believe there was a time she thought twelve thousand in savings was an impressive feat. It was gone, just like that.

It's not like you have much choice if the restaurant is going to stay open, she thought. *Of course, you can always talk to Dad about taking out a loan.*

She nearly laughed at herself. There was no way he'd ever agree—if he was ever even sober enough to have a conversation about it. Besides, that would just make it worse. She'd be in charge of paying it back, with interest.

Might as well use her own savings and avoid the extra charges. Maybe the restaurant would turn around and she'd actually be able to pay herself back.

She locked the door behind the repairman and started prepping for the lunch shift. They only had a one-hour break between breakfast and lunch shifts.

Without a working dishwasher, that was sixty minutes to wash the dishes, cups, and flatware by hand. And of course Dawn demanded her full hour break and Kenzie hadn't come in for the morning shift.

At least you don't have to work at night anymore, she thought to herself as she rolled up her sleeves.

The new hires had actually wanted evening shifts. They were experienced waitstaff and knew that's where the best tips were. Addy knew it too, but it wasn't worth battling it out over the closing shift.

Let them have the heavy tippers, she thought. It made them happy, and happy employees stuck around.

Dawn's timing was impeccable. She showed up for her second shift right as Addy finished up with the last dish.

"Hey! I would have helped if you'd waited for me," she said. She reeked of cigarettes.

"I couldn't wait for you, these needed to be ready for lunch."

Dawn shrugged. "Well ... thanks."

Thanks. Like Addy owed her a favor.

She sucked in her breath to keep from saying anything. The

last thing she needed was for Dawn to quit in a huff and stick Addy with another position to fill.

As Addy headed to the car, her phone buzzed.

"Husband" lit up her screen briefly with a text notification. It made her blush. Before she read the text, she quickly changed it back to "Dr. Hottie."

That was a lot more fitting and not nearly as weird.

If she hadn't shattered that glass of whiskey the other night, she could have really gotten herself in trouble. Jack was just being a guy, and guys didn't turn down sex. Especially not him— God, he must have always had it easy.

Girls throwing themselves at him. Girls like Rosalie, the superwoman-supermodel-superdoctor. She couldn't blame Jack for trying the other night, and she wouldn't have blamed him if they'd taken it farther.

But Addy had to admit to herself that she'd started to develop a serious crush on him. It was manageable if she kept her distance. But if they had sex?

If they'd had sex and then he ended up dumping her for Rosalie in a few weeks when the jealousy scheme worked? It would totally crush her, she knew it.

Isn't that what we're doing this for? So Rosalie will go crawling back to him and Jeremy to me? Is it—is that really what I want?

For the first time, she began to consider that maybe she didn't want Jeremy back. He really was a douche. Maybe it was just her ego that was hurt.

Did I seriously get and stay married because of some bruised ego?

Addy opened up the text as she slid into the driver's seat.

Stop by my work if you have a minute. I have a surprise for you.

A surprise?

She swiftly texted back.

Heading over now, just leaving the restaurant.

It only took ten minutes to reach the hospital.

The benefits of a small town. As soon as she stepped through the doors, she was bombarded with greetings.

"Hi, Mrs. Stratton!"

She blushed every time it was said. She thought she'd get used to it, but it still sounded strange.

Fake. Like everyone was in on it and was just playing along to appease them.

Addy headed back to the ER and immediately spotted Jack as he chatted with a patient who was perched on a table. He caught her eye and nodded.

"Give me a minute," his eyes read.

She smiled. He was absolutely stunning. Beneath the blue scrub bottoms and white coat, it was still easy to make out the perfect physique.

How did he do it? Look so effortlessly gorgeous while working these hours?

She watched as he raked his hand through his hair, perfectly mussed though she knew he put in zero efforts to primping.

"Addy, hi!"

"Hi, Philip," she said. She greeted him with a warm smile.

"How's it going? Here to see the husband?"

"Yeah, I guess so," she said. "How are you? They keeping you busy around here?"

"You have no idea. Well, actually you probably do. Both of our jobs are brutal, huh?"

"I think yours is a little more demanding than mine," she said with a laugh.

Over Philip's shoulder, she caught sight of Rosalie. The glamazon was impossible to miss, especially in an atmosphere like this.

She glided like she was on a runway, a perfect French twist holding her flaxen hair in place. Rosalie chatted with a nurse, the red bud of her mouth plump and full.

Like a French woman, Addy thought. *Effortlessly glamorous with a bun and red lipstick.*

Rosalie must have felt Addy's eyes on her. Her own steel gray eyes snapped up and held Addy's tight. The blonde squinted and slightly frowned.

Addy looked away quickly, back to the warmth of Philip's

friendly gaze. Clearly, Rosalie still struggled with the idea of her being with Jack. Married to Jack.

I guess that's a good thing. That's the goal, right?

"Addy? You okay?" Philip asked.

"Yeah. Sorry! It's been a long day. What were you—"

"Hi, Addison. Good to see you."

Rosalie was suddenly at her side, silent as a cat. She offered up a smile, but it didn't extend all the way to her eyes.

"Rosalie, hi. I was going to come say hello—"

"Oh, it's fine," Rosalie said. "This one is a talker, you'd never get away." She laughed as she nodded at Philip, and he joined in. "Is this your day off? And choosing to spend it in the ER. That's dedication."

"Dedication?"

Before Addy could say anything more, Jack had joined them. He swooped in and greeted Addy with a long kiss.

She kept expecting him to break away, but when he didn't and stretched it out longer, she put her hand on his chest. Jack pulled away and grinned at her, a smile so bright that it melted her insides.

"Hey, love," he said. "Sorry about that. I was just talking to a patient, and guess what?"

"What's that?"

"He said that a restaurant in town is closing, but it's not really public knowledge yet."

"A restaurant? So?" She searched his eyes.

What was he up to now?

"So… they're selling all the furnishings and appliances—"

"Like a dishwasher? Freezer?"

"Yep, just like that. And apparently the owner was friendly with your dad. Rumor has it you can get them both for a song. A Mr. Stills, I think it was?"

"The Stills, yeah, they own that old-fashioned burger joint on the outskirts of town. I can't believe it's closing! But… like, did he say a number?"

"He said around a thousand, give or take."

"A thousand? As in one thousand dollars? That's it? Really?"

Both Rosalie and Philip had disappeared.

"That's right."

Addy launched herself into his arms and hugged him tight. She rested her head on his chest. It felt right, good, like she was home. She hadn't realized how much she'd forced the affection up until this point.

"Hey!" he said with a laugh. "It was no big deal. Just a touch of kismet."

Addy pulled back slightly.

"It is a big deal," she said.

In that moment, with just a few inches of space between them, she felt that flicker again. She felt her eyes begin to droop.

"Again? Get a room!"

One of the nurses walked by and chided them good-naturedly, but it was enough to make Addy remember where they were. And who they were supposed to be.

Jack cleared his throat.

"I'll text you the number he gave me on my next break," he said. "Duty calls. Time to keep up the image of Professional Doctor for a few more hours."

"Thank you," she said. "Seriously. I... I don't know what to say, or how I can repay you."

"I have a few ideas," he said, and wiggled his brows at her.

"Stop it!" she said, and slapped him on the chest.

Part of her was grateful to get back to their normal routine, but another part of her ached for those glimpses of what could be.

"I know. Do you want anything particular for dinner? I have the rest of the day off, so it's doctor's choice. Whatever you want."

"Why don't you surprise me?"

Addy rushed out of the ER, feeling light and giddy. Still, the memory of Jack's touch stayed with her, and she was flushed all the way to the car.

11

"Uh huh," Jack said.

He nodded as his patient, a seventy-two-year-old local woman "born and bred in Genoa" continued to ramble during the assessment.

"And, good heavens, that girl he married? Wouldn't know how to marinate a turkey if her—"

"Mrs. Miller, if we could get back to your symptoms. Where, exactly, does it hurt?"

"Oh, somewhere around here," she said, and gestured loosely at her hip, pelvic, and abdominal area.

"Would you say it's chronic? Acute?"

"Once you get to be my age, it's just normal. You know, when I was younger, I could…"

Jack went about the cursory examination using her physical responses to gauge the problem. He started to zone out and thought about Addy as his years of training took over. She'd surprised him last night with dinner.

The aroma had hit him even before he'd opened the front door. A succulent meat, roasted vegetables, and a hint of something sweet in the oven.

"What did you make?" he asked, and stopped in the doorway when he walked in.

She'd picked up a small dining table and had draped a cream-colored linen tablecloth over it. A bottle of wine chilled in a silver bucket. From across the pony wall bar that separated the living room and kitchen, he'd watched her bustle about with her work face on.

"Lahontan cutthroat trout," she said with a smile. "It's a local fish, recently restocked after commercial fishing almost decimated the population starting in the thirties."

"It smells amazing," he said.

"I hope it tastes as good. Go ahead, sit," she said. "Open the wine, dinner will be ready in ten."

"Can I help with—"

"No, seriously, I got this. I do this all day. You have to be tired. If you want to help, you can pour me a glass, too."

He opened the bottle, poured two glasses, and leaned over the bar to watch her work. Addy had been barefoot, and her curvy thighs shot out of worn khaki shorts she'd rolled up to nearly the crest of her legs.

The kitchen was hot, and the baby hairs that framed her face clung to her dewy skin.

Curves for days, he thought. The tan skin of the tops of her feet were in stark contrast to the pearly white of her at-home pedicure.

He watched as she expertly pulled the seasoned vegetables out of the oven and moved a homemade pie to a rack for cooling. The fish came out last with a gust of rich, buttery aroma.

As she plated their dishes, the steam rose to her face. She whipped out a kitchen towel and cleaned up the plates.

"They don't need to look pretty," he said.

She glanced up at him. "Why not?"

"I guess you're right."

They toasted as they sat across from each other. His mouth had watered as he cut into the flaky, moist fish.

"That's a good sign," she said.

"What?"

"Silence at the dinner table."

"Sorry," he said, his mouth full of the melting fish.

"No, I mean it. It means the food's good."

"It's amazing," he said. "I have to admit I'm surprised."

"Why? I told you I liked cooking."

"Yeah, but a lot of people say that. Doesn't mean they're good at it."

"Thanks for the vote of confidence," she said, but there was a sparkle in her eye.

Jack had looked down and realized his plate was wiped clean.

"More?" she asked. "There are some vegetables left. Or dessert."

"If you're asking me if I want vegetables—which were great, by the way—or that pie you baked, I'm going to have to go with the latter."

She'd smiled, pushed her chair back, picked up both their plates and went into the kitchen. He listened as she pulled out the plates that had appeared in their cupboards the day before and cut into the pie.

"Whipped cream or no?" she'd asked, and leaned against the frame between the kitchen and living room.

A wicked smile played at her face. She held out a bowl of homemade whipped cream, put a finger into the thick cloud of it, and tasted it while she held his gaze.

"Wanna try? Tell me if it's sweet enough."

Okay, maybe that part didn't happen. But if it did—

"Dr. Stratton?" Mrs. Wood's milky blue eyes probed his.

"Oh, uh, sorry," he said. "What did you say?"

"I—"

She suddenly leaned over and vomited blood all over his shoes.

"Don't worry," he said, and his training kicked into overdrive.

One of the nurses arrived at his side.

"Free fluid in the abdomen," he said curtly. "Get Philip—er, Dr. Ruiz."

Philip came through the curtain at a brisk clip and helped prep the patient for surgery.

"I got it," Philip said under his breath to Jack.

Philip's specialty was surgery, and if he was available he

always got priority in the ER. Jack didn't complain—as he moved deeper into internal medicine, he considered this jaunt in the ER a kind of tough initiation with a touch of hazing.

Something to get through before he dug into what he really wanted to do. At least, what he really wanted to do if medicine was the only option.

He stepped back from the exam table and looked down at his shoes as Philip and a nurse wheeled Mrs. Wood to the OR.

"Dr. Stratton?" One of his favorite nurses, Loretta, pulled open the curtains and gave him a kind smile. She handed him a wet wipe and a towel.

"Thanks," he said, and leaned against the counter to wipe off his shoes.

"You bring a spare pair like I told you?" she asked. She crossed her hefty arms across her even more ample chest.

"No, mum, sorry. I forgot," he said.

She tsked at him.

"I've been working the ER for thirty years," she said. "You oughta listen to me when I tell you to keep a spare pair of shoes here."

He grinned up at her, taking note of how her hair wrap perfectly matched her scrubs. How she always wore a different set of oversized, sparkling earrings every day.

"Yeah, you got style, girl," he said. "I could use some lessons."

"Mm-hmm," she said. "Save it for the wifey. Those charms of yours don't work on me."

As she turned and left, his thoughts went immediately back to Addy.

Stop it, he told himself. *All this fantasizing at work is what got this blood and vomit on your shoes to begin with.*

Was his increasing interest in Addy getting in the way of his work? It was the third time he'd been caught zoning out while thinking about her instead of actively engaged in working on a trauma.

She was proving to be a distraction, that was for sure. And that was a lot more than what he'd bargained for. Jack looked at his watch. His shift was up in ten minutes, and there were no signs of a new patient being assigned to him.

Jack started down the hallway toward the staff lounge—only to have Rosalie emerge from the restroom and almost walk smack into him.

"Rosalie, hey," he said. "How's—how's it going?"

"I'm about to start a fourteen-hour shift," she said. "It's going as well as it could be. How's your... wife?" she asked.

"Addison."

"I know what her name is."

"She's fine, thanks for asking," he said.

Rosalie nodded and looked away.

Jack smiled, amused. He hadn't thought their little deception would work so well, but Rosalie clearly struggled with the whole thing. Rosalie was tough, always had been.

That was partly what had initially attracted him to her. He never thought he'd be able to get under her skin so well, and so easily.

"Well, I should let you get started," he said.

"Jack—I, this is awkward," she said. "I think, you know, I have five minutes. Let me just get this out."

"Okay," he said. "Shoot."

She looked up and down the hall, but it was deserted save for one janitor who mopped at the far end.

"I'm... well, it's pretty obvious I'm not happy about the whole thing."

"About me and Addison?"

"Yeah. I'm bitter, I admit it. It's hard, you know? I mean, it kind of came out of nowhere. But I've been working on accepting it. I'm trying to let it go. If we're going to work together, I don't want to have this cloud hanging over us all the time."

"Yeah, I agree," he said.

"So, that's why I was thinking... why don't we double date?"

"What? You mean, Addy and me, and you and..."

"Just someone I recently started dating," she said with a shrug.

"Oh. Who's the new guy?" he asked. He could have kicked himself for his interest.

Rosalie shot him a look. "You aren't allowed to have an opinion about who I date. You're married."

"I know that," he said. She had him there.

"So? Double date tomorrow night? It's probably one of the few times neither of us have the night shift."

"You know my schedule?"

She rolled her eyes at him.

"It's posted in the break room," she said. "I looked when I got here so I could ask you."

"Oh."

"So, dinner tomorrow? Maybe at seven?"

"You've got a date," Jack said.

She smiled and started toward the ER.

As Jack grabbed his bag out of his locker and headed toward the Jeep, he ran over the conversation with Rosalie in his head.

Was she up to something? Or being genuine? He couldn't tell. The Rosalie he knew, or thought he knew, back in the Congo wasn't underhanded or manipulative. At least she hadn't seemed to be.

Maybe she's for real, he thought.

As he walked into the condo, he saw Addy as she prepped for work.

"Dinner shift?" he asked. "I thought you didn't work those."

"Dawn's sick," she said. "I have to cover for her."

"Are you working tomorrow night?"

"No, morning shift. Why?" she asked as she pulled her hair into a ponytail.

"We're going to dinner with Rosalie and some guy she's dating."

"We're what?"

He shrugged. "She asked, said she didn't want things to be weird at work so this is supposed to smooth things over."

"Okay, sounds fun," she said.

"I wouldn't use that word."

"Come on. I thought that's what this was all about? Getting to our exes. What better place than dinner?"

He watched her as she left, purse slung over one shoulder with keys that jangled in her hand.

Sounds fun?

It wasn't just what she said, but how she said it. The response was like what a girlfriend would say. And as much as he was attracted to Addy, he had to remember that this whole marriage thing was just to make Rosalie jealous.

How am I supposed to remind Addy of that? he wondered. *Especially without making her mad—and still convincing her to put on a good show tomorrow night?*

Jack poured himself a glass of whiskey and sat on the patio to mull over his approach.

12

Why did I agree to this?

Addy smoothed down her navy blue dress, nervous as Jack steered the Jeep into the only expensive steakhouse in town. She let go of her hair, which she'd loosely braided to keep her rare blowout from turning into a rat's nest on the drive.

"Ready?" Jack asked.

"I'm nervous," she said.

"You have to be joking."

"I'm not!" she said.

She pulled down the little mirror to check her makeup. It had been so long since she'd actually put in more effort than lip gloss and mascara that she was rusty.

"In that dress, you're making heads turn left and right."

"What are you talking about? We haven't *been* anywhere except home and this parking lot."

"And in that time you about gave the old man in the corner unit a heart attack, and those two teenaged boys who are always hanging out on the front steps something to aspire to."

"Great, so I excited an old man and two hormonal teenage boys who would hump a fire hydrant."

"Wow, learn to take a compliment," he said.

The valet opened her door and held out his white gloved hand. She smiled up at him and grasped it.

Maybe Jack was right.

The valet's eyes nearly bugged out of his head as he took in the extremely low cut of the knit jersey dress. Kenzie had nearly forced it on her, and it was more of a skirt with two really long straps at the waist that lifted up and tied around her neck Grecian-style.

"I don't know," she'd whined at Kenzie, and cupped her bare breasts over the fabric. "This is really out there."

"Well, I know," Kenzie had said. "Trust me. You know what I'd give for a dinner at Stovall's?"

With newfound confidence, she took Jack's hand as he reached for hers and pushed her shoulders back as they walked into the restaurant. Massive chandeliers hung overhead and the rich, red velvet of the booths against the intricate Persian rugs offered a type of immediate, luxurious intimacy.

"Reservations?" the hostess asked.

"Stratton," Jack said. The young hostess couldn't have been older than twenty, too young to be able to control the blatant lust in her eyes.

"Is this a special occasion?" the girl asked. She completely ignored Addy.

"Just a night out with my wife and friends," Jack said.

The waitress shot Addy a look of pure jealousy and looked down to seek out the ring. Addy had to admit it felt good.

If this is what being a power couple is like, I can't complain.

"The other half of the party is already seated. Follow me," the hostess said curtly.

Addy gulped when she saw Rosalie. Jack's ex was seated next to a handsome man with jet black hair combed back.

"Jack, Addy, hi!" Rosalie said when she saw them. She offered up that megawatt grin that punctuated her perfectly lined red lips even more. "This is Theo," she said as the waitress slapped down two cocktail menus and walked away.

Theo stood up to shake their hands. He was tall, Addy noticed, but not quite as tall as Jack. His sharp face was freshly shorn and when he smiled he revealed teeth so perfectly white Addy wondered if they were veneers.

"I've heard a lot about you both," Theo said. "Glad we could all get together. It sounds like all of our schedules are hectic."

"Theo's a producer in Los Angeles," Rosalie said. "He's just in town until tomorrow."

"Wow, that's ... impressive," Addy said as she sat down while Jack pulled out her chair.

Rosalie smiled at her, and for a moment it looked almost genuine. She looked stunning, Addy couldn't help but notice. Rosalie's alabaster skin was contrasted against her aubergine silk top and showed off arms so slender they looked unreal—beautiful in a nearly skeletal way.

She shivered as Jack ran his hand across the bare flesh of her upper back as he took his own seat. As the group began to talk, he wrapped his arm around her like it was the most natural thing in the world.

Jack radiated heat, and she soaked up every bit of it. She didn't know if the chill in the air was from the awkwardness of the situation or just because this was the first time she'd been in a restaurant without working in months.

Are all restaurants this cold?

Addy coasted in and out of the conversation. Jack asked Theo polite questions about his flight and his work, while Rosalie and Jack had the tendency to get caught up in "hospital talk."

Theo raised his eyes at Addy and shook his head with a smile when the doctors got too deep into their jargon.

"So, how did you two meet?" Addy asked. "If you're in California and Rosalie's here."

"I actually have a cabin in Tahoe," Theo said. "It's a convenient getaway from Hollywood, and I love to ski in the winter and enjoy water sports in the summer. That's how we met—I reinjured my rotator cuff on my new jet ski, and Rosalie is the one who fixed me up."

Rosalie laughed.

"Fixed you up is a bit extreme," she said. "More like ordered an MRI and referred you to a surgeon in Los Angeles."

The waiter approached with a polite smile.

"Can I get you started with some drinks?"

"Share a bottle of red?" Jack and Rosalie asked in tandem.

They laughed together and shared what Addy swore was a secret, intimate look.

"Sounds good to me," Theo said, and Addy shrugged at Jack.

"I tend toward Bordeaux blends, but I say Theo chooses since he's the out-of-town guest."

"We'll take the bottle of 2009 Chateau Lafite Rothschild," Theo said. "To start."

Addy pretended to peruse the cocktail side of the menu, but searched for the bottle Theo ordered. She nearly choked at the price—over a thousand dollars.

I'm the only one at this table who doesn't have the potential to make six or seven figures, she realized.

A small part of her deflated. She stared off into space while she partially listened to the conversation around her. Addy didn't have much to contribute to talks about hospital politics or Hollywood productions.

Her breath caught when she saw Jeremy with a lithe blonde on his arm being seated just four tables away—a blonde that wasn't Shannon.

What, did the whole town decide they had to have steak today?

Jeremy caught her eye just as he started to sit. With a grin, he rose back up, grabbed his date's hand, and strolled over to their table.

"What a surprise," Jeremy said. "Addy, I didn't expect to see you somewhere like this. This is Melissa."

"Marissa," the girl corrected.

She tugged self-consciously at her miniskirt that barely covered her ass.

"What happened to Shannon?" Addy asked.

Jeremy shrugged and smiled.

"I can't be tied down. Not ready to walk the marriage plank. No offense," he added, and looked at Jack.

Jack shrugged, apparently unruffled by it.

"Oh, hello!" the waiter said as he appeared with the bottle of wine. "Are we adding two more for dinner?"

Addy opened her mouth, but before she could say anything, Jack jumped in with a resounding, "Yes."

Her jaw dropped and she looked to Jeremy, but he seemed up for the challenge. Before she knew what had happened, the table was shuffled around to squeeze in two more.

Addy squeezed Jack's knee under the table, and he looked at her with a comforting grin. He settled back into his chair, one arm around Addy while he held the wine glass in his other hand.

Across the table, she saw that Jeremy really piled on the PDA with his date. With his arm across Marissa's shoulder, he grazed the side of her breast repeatedly with his thumb. Not to be outdone, Addy curled deeper into Jack's embrace and briefly rested her head on his chest between sips of the admittedly decadent wine.

Rosalie cleared her throat, and it brought Addy back to reality. She'd forgotten about *this* ex in her quest to make Jeremy jealous.

Rosalie was visibly uncomfortable and jealous, but Addy didn't have time to focus on her right now.

Besides, it looks like the Jeremy Challenge is working for her, too.

When the waiter returned, another bottle of wine was ordered but the first glass had made her just tipsy enough to no longer care. Addy was grateful that Jack ordered for her—a bone marrow starter to share and petite filet mignon topped with lobster.

"Excuse me," Rosalie said when the waiter left. "I'll be right back."

"Go to the restroom, too," Jack whispered to her.

"What?"

"Go!" he said under his breath.

"I, um, excuse me," Addy said. Rosalie was already halfway to the restroom.

She wasn't sure what she was supposed to do as she followed Rosalie's retreating back. But as soon as she reached the long hallway that led to the restrooms, she felt a firm hand on her waist.

"What—"

She turned to find Jack behind her, a hunger in his eyes she hadn't seen before. Addy didn't know what he was doing, but he pulled her close and kissed her in a way that nearly knocked the breath out of her.

She felt herself melt into a puddle against him as he pressed her against the wall. His tongue invaded her mouth and she let out a whimper as he dominated her.

Jack pushed himself against her and she was surprised to find he was hard—and very well-endowed.

It was like she was watching someone else, some other couple. She couldn't stop herself. Without thinking, she slid her hand between them and felt the outline of his bulge. A growl erupted low in his throat.

"Excuse me?"

They both turned to see Rosalie one foot away from them, returning from the restroom. The hallway was so narrow she couldn't slip past them.

Jack jumped away from Addy while she wiped her mouth with the back of her hand.

"Sorry," Addy said. Jack grinned at her while Rosalie squeezed by with a scowl and rushed back to their table.

The two of them followed closely. Addy was relieved to find a full glass of wine waiting for her. She downed it in a few swallows. Across the table, Rosalie was red with anger. Addy could almost feel the excitement that emanated from Jack at the sight of the jealousy.

It made him turn up the charm even more. As he refilled Addy's glass, he leaned into her and put his hand on her bare thigh.

"I want to taste you again," he whispered into her ear. She squirmed.

His hand was searing on her skin. Every time she tried to move, his fingers gripped her tighter. Twice, she pushed his hand away, but he returned it each time—and every time, it was a little higher up her leg.

Addy looked to him when the conversation at the table was finally somewhat fluid, and he raised his brow. She took a deep swallow of the wine and picked at her dinner when it arrived.

She couldn't help but notice Jeremy's eyes on her, amused.

You can't let him win, she told herself.

Addy scooted her chair closer to Jack. When the table started to finish up dinner, she let out a small yawn and snuggled up to him with her hand on his chest. Addy sneaked a look at Jeremy, who still stared at her. The smirk was gone.

"Can I interest anyone in dessert?" the waiter asked while a busboy discreetly cleared the table and swiped up the crumbs.

Addy elbowed Jack in the ribs.

It's time to go, she tried to tell him without words.

"Actually, we have to be going," Jack said.

He dropped a stack of bills on the table and winked at Rosalie. Addy's vision was swimming just enough that she couldn't tell how much money he'd left. As they rose, Jack pulled out Addy's chair once again and helped her up.

He escorted her toward the door, but just before they were out of sight he stopped and pulled her close once again for a passionate kiss. Even with her eyes closed, she could feel the eyes that seared into them from the table.

Once they were finally outside, Addy breathed out a sigh of relief while the cool night air enveloped her.

"Thank God we don't have people to fool at home. Dinner wore me out."

Jack looked at her questioningly and brushed the valet aside to open the door for her himself.

What is he thinking?

13

Must be my lucky night, Jack thought as he slipped into the on-call sleep room.

For once, there was nobody else in there and he had his pick of the pair of bunk beds. He climbed onto the top of the one closest to the window and barely got the thin blanket over himself before sleep claimed him.

"Jack."

Addy stood in the doorway that led from their hallway to the living room. Suddenly it was the couch he was sleeping on, not the creaking hospital bed.

Dimly aware that it was a dream, he clung to it tight. She wore nothing but those khaki shorts she'd rolled up the first night she cooked him dinner and a paper-thin white tank top he could clearly see her hard, pale pink nipples through.

"Can't sleep?" he asked. His cock sprung to attention and shifted the blanket.

Addy shook her head and ran her hand across her breasts. "I had a dream."

"About what?"

"You," she said, almost shy.

"What happened? A sex dream?"

"Yeah…"

"Tell me about it."

"You were... eating my pussy. And I was so close, but ..."

"Come here."

As she bit her lip, she pulled the tank top over her head. Addy hooked the shorts through her thumbs and wiggled them off her hips. As she strode toward him, he was hypnotized by the sway of her hips, how they splayed upward to her tiny chest.

Jack's head was on the swell of the couch arm. He couldn't move. Addy's thigh brushed his cheek as she approached, wearing just a pair of baby blue panties.

As she stood over him, she pulled each side of the thin lace strings up high and showed him the dark blue wetness of the material's crotch.

"Look what you did to me," she said.

He regained movement in his body as his cock ached with want. Jack grabbed her ass cheeks, bare in the thong, and pulled her to his face to kiss her center through the fabric. As Addy let out a cry, he tore the panties off her.

"Sit on my face," he commanded.

Addy angled herself to stand over the couch and straddled his face. As soon as his lips met her sticky sweetness, she started to gush. He watched her tits bounce above him and her long fingers pull at her nipples while she ground against him.

"Fuck me, please," she started to moan. "Please, Jack, I need you inside me."

His fingers gripped tight into her thick ass as he controlled her bouncing on his tongue. When she was close to coming, he lifted her off and directed her toward him.

Greedily, Addy climbed onto him. With her hands on his chest, she started to ride. Her head was tilted back and that long hair grazed his legs—

"Dr. Stratton?"

Jack groaned against the sudden light.

"You're up. They need you in the ER, room 1-B." The nurse walked away at a fast clip.

Jack scrambled to the bathroom, leaned against the wall, and jerked himself off in less than thirty seconds—thoughts of Addy riding him skyrocketed him to orgasm. He stifled his cry and wiped up before he downed another 5-hour Energy shot, his second of the shift.

Shifts, he corrected himself. He couldn't believe it was her he dreamed of and not Rosalie.

"Glad you could join us," Rosalie said as Jack opened 1-B.

As she started to bark orders and update him on the patient, he couldn't stop looking at her.

What was it about her that's so goddamned attractive, anyway? he wondered.

Sure, she was beautiful. And smart as hell. But ... something was different. He was different. In that moment, while Rosalie and her perfect lip liner loomed over the teenage boy with the fractured ulna, he knew he didn't want her back.

Well. That puts you in a fucking weird place, doesn't it? He knew he had to tell Addy. *But how the hell does that conversation go?*

The rest of his shift went blessedly fast. It was eight o'clock when he finally clocked out, and the summer sun still lingered in the sky. He didn't know if he could handle seeing her, just the two of them, after that dream.

Up for drinks? Addy's text popped up on his screen.

Talk about perfect timing, he thought.

Sure. Half the bottle of whiskey's still there, he replied.

Surely he could handle a couple of minutes in the same room with her without thinking about ripping off her clothes and seeing if she was really that sweet. Right?

I was thinking of going out. Want to meet up with some friends for drinks? That place on Pine? she asked.

Sure. Now? I can drive straight there.

See you there, she replied.

Jack didn't care if this meant he had to show up at a bar in his work clothes. At least he wouldn't have temptation right in his face at home without even a nip to dull the ache.

When he showed up at the country bar, he immediately spotted Addy. She sat right next to Jeremy at a table crowded with faces he vaguely recognized. As Addy threw her head back and laughed at something Jeremy said, she touched his arm lightly.

Jack couldn't stop the scowl that spread across his face, but when she saw him she lit up and scooted over. Addy patted the seat between her and Jeremy.

She's one hell of an actress, he thought. She seemed genuinely happy to see him.

He sat down, hyperaware that he'd just cut some insane tension between the two of them. Jeremy gave him a dark glower.

"I need another round," Jeremy growled and headed to the bar.

"Hey, everyone!" Addy called to the group. "This is my husband, Jack!"

His heart soared at the word "husband" and gave him the boost he needed to fake it through the night. Addy went around and ticked off names he'd never remember. It was fairly obvious everyone was pretty tipsy, including Addy.

"We're playing Never Have I Ever," Addy explained to Jack. "Do you know it? Do they play it down there?"

"In Australia? Yeah, I'm pretty sure everyone in the world knows that game," he said.

Addy poured him a beer from the shared pitcher. Her buzz made her unaware of his tone.

As she leaned forward to push the pitcher back to the center, Jack caught sight of what she wore. A short plaid skirt, black knee socks, and a tight black t-shirt. The Catholic schoolgirl homage showed off her figure perfectly.

It also didn't hurt that her height, barely five foot three, made the schoolgirl fantasy even more plausible. He shifted as his cock started to harden again.

He'd have her leave the knee socks on, and the skirt at least for a little while ...

The girl seated two people down from Addy held up her hand.

"Okay, okay! Now that we've all met 'Dr. Hottie,' can we get back to it? Never have I ever... joined the mile high club."

Jack drank automatically, his college years kicking in. It

wasn't until he lowered his glass that he realized nobody else had drank and all eyes were on him.

"What? I have my pilot's license. It's kind of a requirement." He winked at Addy and she went pink. The blushing made her irresistible.

How else can I fluster her?

The girl next to Addy pretended to think.

"Hmm," she said. "Never have I ever filmed myself having sex."

Jack took a drink, as did two of the girls at the table.

"Here's to Snapchat!" one of them called, but Addy grew a shade closer to crimson.

"Addy?" Jack asked. "It's your turn."

She tucked her hair behind her ears and gave him a hard look.

"Never have I ever had a threesome."

Jack drank, as did one girl at the far end of the table.

"It was two girls!" she hollered.

"Same here," Jack said.

The guys at the table laughed, but Addy shifted uncomfortably when he wouldn't break his gaze with her.

"Never have I ever had a fivesome," Jack said, and tossed his arm around her. "Yet."

The group lit up with whoops. Addy was hot to the touch, but she didn't resist when he pulled her closer.

"Never have I ever ridden someone's face," the girl on the other side of Jack said. "I'm vanilla. What can I say?"

Instantly, he was back in his dream. Addy had been completely naked and blissed out. He'd never seen her just let go like that before. Her hands pressed against her thighs as she rode his face with her eyes closed.

What I would give to make her feel like that, he thought.

The sound of Addy putting her empty glass down beside him knocked him back to reality. His eyes widened.

She drank?

"You?" he hissed under his breath as the game continued around them. "You're surprising me, Addison," he said. "I didn't think you were that kind of girl. Straddling someone's face, letting him suck on your clit. Licking up your come while you grind against his mouth."

The more explicit he got in the description, the deeper she blushed.

Seeing her blush like that was almost as good as seeing the flush of an afterglow. Almost. Maybe she wasn't as innocent as he thought.

Hell, we're married, he thought. *As long as she consents, I can do just about anything to her.*

As the game moved on, Jack sat back and looked at Addy in a new light. Before the round could come back to her, she stood up abruptly.

"Excuse me," she said.

He watched her head toward the restroom and waited a minute before he followed.

The restrooms were individual and private. And only one was marked "Occupied."

Jack waited outside the door. As soon as she emerged, he pushed her back in and locked the door behind him.

"What are you doing?" she gasped.

"Whatever you want. Unless you want me to leave?"

He knew it was a risk. In the dim light of the bathroom, lit with just one pink bulb, he saw her pupils dilate.

Addy's eyes went to his mouth. She licked her lips. It was just the invitation he needed. Jack closed in on her for the kiss, hard and demanding. She made a soft sound and melted against him.

As he backed her up against the wall, he started to kiss her neck. One hand under her skirt, he searched briefly for the panties—the little blue thong—but found nothing. She had to have been sitting on that wooden barstool with her pussy pressed, warm and wet, right against the wood.

"Naughty girl," he whispered as his fingers grazed the tiny strip of hair highlighted by what had to be a very recent Brazilian wax.

Frenzied, she began to unbutton his pants while he stroked

her clit, already swollen and slick with want. Jack lifted her onto the tiny counter and Addy spread her legs eagerly.

Jack gripped her ankles and pushed her feet onto the counter as her shoes dropped to the floor. With her knees pointed toward the ceiling and her thighs spread wide, he stepped back for a moment to take her in. Those knee-high socks framed her displayed center perfectly.

"Damn," he said and she reached for him. He slid two fingers into her right as she grasped his cock.

A knock came at the door, sharp and hard.

"Ignore it," Jack said. He curled a finger deep inside her and watched her eyes roll back as he hit her G-spot.

"Addy! Are you in there?"

"Fuck, it's Kenzie!" Addy said.

"Addy! Jeremy said you were back here. Are you okay?"

Addy pushed him away and jumped down from the counter.

"I... I had too much to drink," she mumbled to him.

Jack stood back, amazed as Addy straightened her clothes and opened the door with a smile.

"Jesus, Addy," he said, and hurried to shut the door so he could zip up his pants.

What kind of fucking luck is this? he wondered.

Her wetness still coated his fingers. Jack put a finger in his mouth and tasted her. She was even more decadent than he'd imagined. Addictive.

If she was attracted to him, and he was pretty damn sure she was, he'd convince her to act on it sooner or later.

14

She could feel the stiffness of two days' worth of double shifts as soon as she opened her eyes.

But it was worth it, she thought.

Two nights ago, she and Jack had been close to fucking in a bar bathroom. By signing up for those double shifts, she'd avoided him completely since then.

Addy listened closely, but the rest of the condo seemed to be silent. They hadn't spoken since that night. A couple of cursory nods when they passed each other coming or going in the living room had been the only contact they'd had.

Now, the condo sounded empty.

She couldn't stop replaying what had happened in that bathroom in her head. It had consumed her during each of those eighteen-hour shifts.

Thank God waiting tables didn't take much concentration after a certain point, she thought.

She'd been on autopilot, but it was good to keep her hands busy.

Huh. Is it weird to masturbate in his bed? she wondered.

Addy slid a hand down her taut belly and below her underwear. With knees drawn up and thighs spread open, she surprised herself by how wet she already was. A couple of light flicks across her clit, and she heard her breathing grow ragged.

"Jack," she whispered, and the memory of his cock, hard and hot in her hand, rushed to her memory.

"Fuck." She pushed away the blankets and sat up.

Would they actually have done it that night? Probably.

It had been nearly impossible to stop herself even when she'd heard Kenzie's voice on the other side of the door. That ache she'd had for him, deep in her center, had stayed with her ever since.

"Stay busy," she told herself.

Addy glanced at the clock. It was almost nine o'clock in the morning. Too late to call into the restaurant and pick up another shift. She had a lot of hours in the day to fill.

She flopped onto the couch and popped open her laptop. At least it would be a little easier to avoid the temptation of getting herself off when she wasn't in bed. She opened Facebook and got a whiff of Jack's cologne.

Of course the couch would smell like him, she thought. But she straightened her back and trudged forward—directly to his Facebook page.

Addy could tell the page had been carefully cultivated, but it wouldn't be obvious to anybody else. There were scores of pictures of them together.

One photo, the one taken right after the glider trip, had a boosted comment from one of Jack's friends about throwing them a reception to celebrate. She didn't know who the guy was, but he made a good point.

If this was a real marriage, wouldn't it be weird if they never had a reception or party with their friends to celebrate the elopement?

She turned it over in her mind. Addy pictured the perfect white dress. Maybe they could even have another ceremony in town? A more traditional one. She could see herself as she walked down the aisle, Ed Sheeran's "Perfect" performed by a string quartet.

In her mind, she walked alone. That stung briefly, for just a moment, but even in sheer fantasy she couldn't fathom her father getting it together enough to walk her down the aisle.

Jack would be waiting at the end in a sharp tuxedo, that smile across his face that made her wobble—

Stop it. You're being ridiculous.

Addy sighed. She really was. It was clear even to her that this fantasy was more about a wedding and less about making sure their little ploy was believable. *But is it about the wedding, or the marriage?*

Her phone vibrated against her thigh and brought her back to reality.

I'm getting relieved from on-call duties this evening, be home for dinner, Jack texted.

Is he going to act like nothing had happened? After two days of silence? she thought.

Sounds good, she texted back. It was already almost four in the afternoon.

Shit. Did I really spend all freaking day on Facebook and fantasizing about weddings? Addy jumped up and threw herself into making a lasagna. *Thank God for a stocked kitchen.*

It had been one of the tasks besides work in the past two days to keep her busy and away from possibly running into Jack.

She preheated the oven and put on a pot of water to boil. Addy warmed olive oil and browned ground beef in a saucepan, then added garlic and oregano. As she added in the marinara, salt and pepper, she drained the cooked noodles and drizzled a touch of olive oil across them to prevent sticking.

This was her zone, in the kitchen and surrounded by food.

I should have relieved one of the cooks instead of busting my ass on tables the past two days.

Addy pulled out one of the heavy glass bowls from the cupboard and began to combine the ricotta, parmesan and parsley. She layered the sauce, noodles, and cheese in a casserole dish precisely and expertly. Even in her rush, she saw that it was restaurant quality.

"Perfect," she whispered as she opened the oven door to start baking.

Addy almost dropped the entire dish as her phone rang in her shorts pocket. Kenzie.

"Kenzie? Everything okay?" she asked as she put the phone on speaker and set it on the counter.

"No," Kenzie said quietly. She could hear the tremble in her voice. "It's Dad—"

"What happened?" Addy pulled the phone to her ear. "Is he okay?"

"He's... distraught," Kenzie said.

"Distraught. What does that mean? What happened?"

"He won't get out of his chair. Can you... come help?" Kenzie used the little girl voice that always worked on everyone in the family.

"Kenzie! Is he breathing? Is he alright? Do you need to call an ambulance—"

"Yes! He's breathing, he's alive, if that's what you're asking. God, do you think I'd call you if I thought he was dead?"

"I don't know, Kenzie! Yes? Probably."

"Wow, thanks! But seriously, Addy, he's really out of it." *Really drunk, you mean.* "Can you please just come help? I know you had the whole day off—"

Addy gritted her teeth. "I—fine. Yes, okay. I'll be there soon."

Addy hung up, slammed the oven door, and set the timer for twenty minutes. That was one of the perks of Jack renting at the best complex in town. Fancy kitchen gadgets with automatic timers. She pulled a sticky pad out of the junk drawer and started to scribble a note to Jack.

"Hey." Addy nearly jumped out of her skin at his voice.

"Jack! I didn't hear you come in. I was just leaving you a note—"

"What's wrong?"

"Nothing," she said defensively. "Why?"

"Addy, I can tell you're upset. What's wrong?"

She sighed. "It's my dad—"

"Is he okay?"

"Yeah, sure. If you consider drunk and passed out okay. Kenzie just called, she wants me to go over there and help."

"I'm going with you." He looked exhausted in wrinkled scrubs.

"No, stay. Dinner will be ready in twenty, so just help yourself to—"

"Addison. I'm going with you."

Something in his voice told her not to argue. She let him usher her toward the door as visions of what they were walking into raced through her head.

"Jack, my dad doesn't even know you. What will I say? Honestly, I don't even know how much he knows about our whole… situation."

"We'll read the situation when we get there," Jack said calmly. "I'll just be your doctor friend if he doesn't know."

Jack opened the passenger door for her. It overwhelmed her, all of it. He didn't have to be so kind to her. She leaned up and hugged him close. But the scent of him, the nearness of him, knocked her right back to the bar bathroom.

"Let's, um… let's go," she said.

He'd barely parked in the driveway before she had the door open and rushed up the stairs. The front door was open, as always. It looked like Kenzie had every light in the house on.

"Dad! Come on, let go!" Kenzie cried from the living room.

Addy rushed toward the sound, faintly aware of Jack's footsteps behind her. Kenzie leaned over the recliner and tried to pry a bottle of whiskey out of their father's hands.

Instantly, Addy was embarrassed.

I shouldn't have let Jack come.

She saw her whole messed up family in a new light. Even from feet away, she could tell her dad smelled awful. He obviously hadn't showered or eaten a decent meal since she'd moved in with Jack.

God. Have I really not seen him since then?

Her dad rolled his eyes toward Addison. *Well. At least he's awake.*

"You," he stammered. "What the fuck are you doing here?"

"I called her, Dad," Kenzie said.

She took his distraction as an opportunity to finally wrench the bottle from his hands.

"I don't need *you* interfering in my life," her dad growled at her.

She frowned at him, but he wasn't about to start taking her social cues.

"Ungrateful. Just up and leave us when we need you—who's this?" he asked, finally aware of Jack.

"I'm Jack Stratton," Jack said calmly. "I'm a doctor at the new hospital."

"A doctor, huh?" her dad asked as he eyed him. "Well, good for you."

"Mr. Fuller, do you mind if I ask you a few questions? Do a basic checkup?"

Addy was shocked her father didn't immediately object. Instead, he looked at Addy and Kenzie carefully.

"Since you're already here…" her dad said.

"Addy, Kenzie? Do you mind giving us some privacy?" Jack said.

It wasn't really a question.

Kenzie gripped Addy's arm as they bolted out of the living room.

"Oh my God, thank God you're here," Kenzie said. "I didn't know—"

"How could you let him get this bad?" Addy demanded.

She shook Kenzie's grip off her arm.

Kenzie blinked. "He's an adult, you know …"

Addy hung her head. She felt betrayed—and responsible.

Of course Kenzie didn't take care of him. You knew she wouldn't. What the hell were you thinking?

"Kenzie," she said slowly. "I came back here, dropped out of college, to take care of things so they wouldn't turn out *exactly* like they are right now. It's only been a few weeks, and… and…"

She stopped as her dad walked straight through the kitchen, took a water out of the fridge, and continued to the back of the house toward his bedroom.

"What the…" Kenzie started.

Jack followed close behind. "Your dad is going to take a

shower," he said. "Then all of us are heading back to my, uh, our place, for dinner."

"Dinner? But I had plans..." Kenzie started to complain. Addy shot her a look that shut her up immediately.

Good to know the big sister warning shot still works.

"How did you do that?" Addy asked. "What did you say to him?"

"I've been trying to get him to just sit up for days," Kenzie said.

"It's nothing," Jack said.

The three of them hovered in the kitchen in silence as they listened to the sound of the shower running.

"All set!" her dad said.

He appeared in the kitchen freshly showered in a button-up shirt and jeans. His eyes were still bloodshot and there were burst vessels across his nose, but it was the nicest—and soberest—she'd seen him in years.

"Let's take two cars," Jack said. "Kenzie, you mind driving your dad?"

Addy kept an eye on the headlights behind them as they wound toward the condo. There were a million questions she wanted to ask Jack, but none of them managed to make their way out.

As soon as the four of them stepped into the condo, they were hit with the rich, hearty aroma of a perfectly crafted lasagna.

She was nervous as she served the table and kept an eagle eye on her father. He behaved perfectly, though she kept waiting for his usual drunken self to emerge.

It was something about Jack, she realized. It had her dad on his best behavior.

"This is amazing, Addy," Kenzie said. "Seriously, we should add this to the menu."

"Good stuff, kid," her dad said. He sat beside her and smelled like his old self, of Old Spice aftershave and Dove soap. Like how he used to smell when Mom was alive. "You know, you should find yourself someone like Jack, here," he said.

Addy shot a look to Kenzie.

Really? She hadn't told their dad? Kenzie's eyes widened to feign innocence.

"I think your daughter's doing pretty good," Jack said quickly.

Addy hurried to clean up the plates as they finished up. "Kenzie, it's getting late. Maybe you should get Dad home?"

Kenzie looked at her phone.

"Yeah, I have something to get to tonight, anyway," she said. "Come on, Dad. I'll take you home."

For once, Kenzie's social life worked in my favor.

It felt strange to hug her dad goodbye, but for a second it felt like the old days.

"Need some help washing?" Jack asked.

"Sure," she said with a shrug. "Just need to get the cheese off, mostly. The dishwasher will take care of the rest."

She stole glances at him beside her at the sink. When she checked to make sure the table was clear, she returned to his broad back bent over the farmhouse sink while he scrubbed away at the casserole pan. Overwhelmed, she embraced him from behind.

"Thank you for today," she whispered.

He started to turn. Before she could get herself into trouble, she ran off to her room.

15

Jack poured the creamer generously into the thick coffee mug emblazoned with Addy's family's restaurant logo. He sprinkled in two spoonfuls of Splenda and swirled the sweet concoction.

From the bedroom doorway, he paused. She was beautiful when she slept, innocent and unconcerned. It was the only time he ever saw her without worries visibly dotted across her face.

Addy was sprawled across the bed with one tanned leg slung over the sheet. Her t-shirt had inched up during the night to expose a stretch of her toned stomach.

With each deep breath, he couldn't help but notice the rise and fall of her chest. Clearly braless, for a moment he almost thought he could see through the white material.

"Morning," he said, just as his arousal started to shift in his scrubs.

"Morning," she murmured, eyes still closed. Slowly, she opened them and squinted. "Is that coffee?"

"With creamer and Splenda, just like you like. You know, those fake sweeteners will kill you," he said with a smile as he moved toward her outstretched hands.

"So will a morning without coffee," she said before she took a sip. "Okay, you got my attention. And now I know you want something. What's up?"

Jack grinned. "Get up. Get dressed. The stars have magically aligned, and we both have the day off."

She groaned. "Do I have to?"

"Yes, doctor's orders. And wear workout clothes or something."

"We're working out? No, I don't think so," she said and put the coffee on the nightstand. "No coffee is worth that."

"We're not working out. But wear something you don't mind getting dirty."

"What?"

Before she could argue, he left the room and shut the door.

"What are we doing?" she called behind him.

"It's a surprise! Hurry up," he yelled from the living room.

Twenty minutes later, she appeared in the living room freshly showered wearing black yoga pants and a heathered gray Santa Fe University top with a generous V-neck. A strappy black sports bra could be seen underneath.

"Okay, I'm ready. Now tell me," she said.

"Everything's in the car. You'll see."

She groaned, but let him grab her hand and drag her toward the Jeep. Addy peeked in the back, but all she could make out were duffel bags.

"Are we going on a hike?" she asked. She slipped on a pair of aviators and stuffed her hair under a baseball cap.

"Quite the opposite, actually. But that's all the hint you get," he said. "Here, eat this," he said as he handed her a meal replacement bar. "You'll need it."

From the corner of his eye, he watched her break off pieces by hand and chew slowly. Jack checked the distance. They were getting closer. Soon, signs for Black Chasm Cavern started to appear. He watched her take them in and shot him a curious look.

Jack pulled into a gravel lot.

"Come on," he said. "We're going spelunking."

"No way," she said.

Addy shook her head vehemently, but took the blue jumpsuit

he handed her. She stepped into the belay belt and warily took the red helmet he handed her from the bag.

"Don't worry," he said. "You're in good hands."

As he hoisted the belt over her hips and cinched it tight at her groin, he couldn't help himself. Being this close to her, his hands inches from that sweetness he'd been teased with.

Addy audibly gulped. Jack looked up from where he squatted before her and saw a deep blush spread across her face.

"Let's go," he said, and gave her belt one final test tug.

He led the way into the first cavern and gestured for her to turn her light on.

"I didn't know real spelunking, or whatever you call it, was allowed in here," she said. "I thought it was like a tourist trap."

"From what I could tell, it isn't allowed," he said.

"Jack!"

"Don't worry," he said. "I did my research. Lots of people sneak in for a little private caving."

As they rounded a corner, he held up a flashlight to the first formation he'd read about.

"Check this out, it's an aeolian."

"What's that?" She came up behind him, mildly breathless from the touch of fear the darkness tends to bring.

"It was created by the wind." Jack turned off the handheld light and slipped it into his pocket. Only the lights on their helmets illuminated the whirling pattern.

"Come on," he said. He couldn't see her hand, but he felt it and she grasped him tight.

"Where are we going?" she said. Addy whispered it, the sacredness of the cave omnipresent.

"The first belay bolt."

He helped her up the first minor ascent and then scrambled after her. In the oily darkness of the little perch, the sediment walls pressed in around them.

He felt like kissing her. She smelled of flowers every time he got close.

The rest of the morning unfolded with plenty of close calls.

Once, in the dark zone of the cavern where daylight could never reach, he almost couldn't stop himself.

He came close, crouched down to avoid the low overhang. Addy didn't need to duck at all. Instead, she looked up at him, her chin tilted upward and those plush lips nearly begged him to close the distance between them.

Yet he resisted.

This was a stupid idea, he realized as they made their way through the tightest quarters of the cavern.

It required them to be on hands and knees. Addy moved ahead of him, her heart-shaped ass punctuated by the outline of the belt. He steadied his breath but couldn't look away.

It took all his willpower not to grasp that belt, pull her back to him, rip off her clothes and sink his hardness deep inside her. With every inch she moved forward on hands and knees, he grew harder.

As they cleared the tunnel, she glanced back at him over her shoulder. Only his headlight illuminated her face.

Ask me to take you, right here, he thought.

But she didn't. She only smiled and stood up, brushing her knees with her fingertips.

"Oh, wow," she said. "What's that called?"

Addy pulled out her own flashlight to illuminate the swirling column.

"Helictite," he said. "They're amazing, aren't they?"

He prayed she wouldn't shine the light down and see his raging hard-on. Jack had never been so thankful for the darkness.

"Thank you for bringing me here," she said quietly.

She reached for his hand and wove her fingers through his easily. It should have been romantic, but it was beyond that. Jack had seen many things in his life, incredible things, but with Addy he saw them with fresh eyes—her eyes.

Had he come alone or with anyone else, he would have simply ticked it off as another helictite featured in one of his many adventures. She made it different, special. She showed him the wonders right in front of him.

He let her lead the way and choose the next fork. As he watched her ass sashay in front of him and her hips swing side to side, he tried to figure it out. He'd never obsessed about a girl so much in his life.

But she's not just any girl, is she?

All the others had basically thrown themselves at him. Even Rosalie. He was used to all the games they tried, whether they were flirty or aloof. The ones like Rosalie who were skilled at playing hard to get were still easy to read.

Rosalie had slept with him on the third date and swore she'd never done anything like that before.

But not Addy. She wasn't like any of them. It was refreshing, and strange, especially after he'd been awarded his MD title. The girls came easily enough before that, but afterward? Even a hint that he was a doctor made the most exquisite of women flock to him.

Why was Addy immune to it?

If anything, she seemed to be the one trying to keep everything light and breezy.

Fuck. If this is a game, she's better at it than I am.

Had he met his match? He couldn't tell. But Addy's seeming indifference to him made him want her even more. And that little incident in the bathroom? He couldn't be totally certain that she would have fucked him had Kenzie not interrupted.

She's so quick to switch gears, she could have called it quits at any minute.

In front of him, she leaned down to squeeze through another small space. Jack reached out, desperate for just a touch of her. To feel her ass in his hands again. Just like that night in the bathroom.

Just like his dream when she let him cradle her cheeks in his hands while she rode his face, demanded with her body that he tongue her clit generously before he dipped it into her center. "Fuck me, please."

He still remembered Dream Addy and how she'd begged for it, even while knowing she was in control. She could have asked anything of him.

"Is that the sun?" Her voice in real time broke his trance.

"Looks like it," he said. Jack commanded his erection to subside by the time they reached the exit. "Stop."

She turned. "What is it?"

"You can't just go out in the sun like that. You have to stay here a minute, let your eyes readjust."

They leaned against the cool walls of the cave, half in the darkness they'd just shared and half in the sun. Addy squinted into the sunlit greenery. She turned to him and opened her mouth. *Just one word, and I'm yours,* he thought.

"I could use a beer," she said, and stretched overhead.

"Yeah, okay. Let's find a bar," he said, deflated.

No matter how hard he tried, he couldn't stop eye fucking her.

16

"Does that sound too serial killer?" she asked.

Addy pointed to the first highway sign for food that they passed after spelunking.

"Noah's Ark Burgers and More? No, not at all," Jack said.

She was exhausted. Addy leaned the seat back and pressed her palms against her thighs. There was a dull burn where the belt had dug into her skin. Still, it had been worth it.

She'd never felt so alive in her life. And being with Jack in the dark, the sexual tension between them, the way she'd felt his eyes on her ass every time she was in front of him—it had been intoxicating.

Addy kept waiting for him to kiss her, to throw her against the wall, to do anything at all, but he'd behaved the entire time.

It wasn't just the spelunking that had exhausted her. Waiting, maddeningly so, for him to make a move was even worse. She thought she'd explode by the time they'd reached the exit.

What, does he think I didn't notice him checking me out all day? Does he think I didn't do the same every time he looked away?

She shook her head and stared out where her window should have been as Jack exited toward the macabrely named burger joint.

You need to get it together, she told herself.

What did she expect? For him to slam her against a cave wall and fuck her wildly in the dark?

Well, maybe, she thought. Even the idea of it got her wet and she squirmed in the seat. *But he's such a classic bad boy. And such a bad life decision.*

The little restaurant was decorated with a huge mural of an ark. Happy animals, two by two, climbed onboard.

"What are they so happy about?" Jack murmured. "Cows, pigs… all the animals they probably serve in there on a bun."

"No penguin, I hope," Addy said.

She pointed to the black and white cartoon animals. He chuckled, but it wasn't enough to cut the tension between them.

Fortunately, the menu was pretty all-American basic. They ordered two cheeseburgers with a basket of tater tots to share. Ice cold beers arrived with the made-to-order lunch and Addy pounced on it, famished.

At least I can feed one kind of hunger, she thought. The cheese melted onto her fingers. She sucked it off greedily.

"Hey," Jack whispered.

"Don't give me any crap," she murmured. Addy didn't take her eyes off the burger. "I'm hungry, okay?"

"No, not that. Look."

Addy looked up and Jack gestured with his eyes toward the other side of the restaurant. "What?"

"See that old couple? They've been staring at us. Maybe this is one of those serial killer towns," he stage whispered.

Addy realized it was an old couple from her hometown. The two who were always in the soda shop for the early bird breakfast special. She couldn't recall their names, but she knew they were huge gossips. It was all they had to do.

"Oh, God," she said. Addy dropped the burger and buried her head in her hands.

"What? Hey, watch it. You're going to get cheese in your hair." Jack leaned across the table and swatted her hands away from her face.

"I know them," she said.

"You do?"

"Well, not really. They're the town gossips. I'm sure they're taking notes, ready to report back everything they see."

"Oh. Well, then let's give them something to talk about."

Quickly, Jack moved to her side of the booth and wrapped his arm around her. He brushed his lips against her ear and instant goosebumps spread across her skin.

He cupped her chin in his hand and forced her face upward. Limp in his arms, she opened her mouth slightly for his kiss. It was warm, pillowy, and simultaneously familiar and exotic.

Addy melted into it, even though she was aware it was for show. But she couldn't help herself. She wanted more. She clutched at his shirt and pulled him closer, opened her mouth to welcome his tongue against hers.

Jack obliged and explored her mouth. He moved to her jawline and inched toward her neck. As she started to make those little animal noises in his ear, he felt his cock stiffen.

She felt his hand graze against her breast while her nipple hardened to attention. There was almost nothing between her nipple, which begged for his kisses, and his fingers. Just two flimsy pieces of fabric.

She wanted more than anything to press herself against his touch. To encourage his hands to roam freely. Open her legs so he could feel how she'd started to soak through those yoga pants at his touch.

But Addy fluttered her eyes open and saw that the old couple had already left.

Should I tell him? No, she thought. *Just one more minute. Just give me one more minute...*

Addy closed her eyes and let herself respond to his touch. He was buried in her neck, and as she pressed her breast against his hand she felt a sting as he started to suck her skin.

Already, she knew he'd leave a mark. It made her wetter, knowing she'd be branded as his.

Through her t-shirt, he pinched her nipple lightly. She responded with a moan loud enough that it broke through her consciousness. Addy didn't care, pushed closer against him.

He pulled at her nipple through the material and she parted

her legs. But Jack's hand stayed at her breast. Frustrated, she reached for his crotch. He was swollen, hard, about to burst through the fabric.

The feel of it shot her into a frenzy. She wanted him, needed him, right then.

Who gives a damn if it's the middle of a restaurant?

"Hey," he said suddenly. "Whoa."

She opened her eyes to see him pulled back. He panted slightly, flushed, but at least he had the wherewithal to keep both of them in check.

"Uh, sorry," she said. Reluctantly, she pulled away. "I guess I just… got carried away with the whole thing."

"It's okay," he said.

The waitress promptly arrived with the bill and gave them both a hard look.

Shit. Noah's Ark. This is probably a super-Christian mom and pop place.

Addy shifted her weight awkwardly while Jack paid the bill.

"Ready?" he asked.

She nodded silently and followed him to the car, head down like a child caught doing something naughty.

"What's wrong?" he asked as they merged back onto the highway.

"What's wrong? You know, we don't need to touch each other or act all cutesy unless Rosalie or Jeremy are around."

"What the hell?" his voice trailed off. She watched a dark cloud settle across his face. "Fine," he said. "You're right."

He stared out the windshield and Addy discreetly inched away so her back faced him. The drive home was long and silent.

She commanded herself not to squirm, no matter how uncomfortable the sticky wetness between her thighs had become.

17

"Thank you for unloading the dishwasher," Addy said formally.

Jack sighed. It had been days since their spelunking adventure, followed by the makeout disaster at that weird restaurant, and the tension was palpable between them. Addy was trying so hard to keep things "friendly but separate" that the whole situation had become incredibly awkward.

And it's my fault, Jack thought.

"Hey, what do you think about a hike this afternoon?" he asked.

"A hike?"

He heard the falter in her voice, but he wasn't surprised. Hiking wasn't totally out of the realm of caving, and they both knew how that had turned out.

"I mean, I'm off at four today, so I just thought…"

"Great! I mean, yeah, a hike sounds good," she said cheerfully.

"Okay, good. I… I guess I'll pick you up a little after four then."

When Jack arrived back at the condo, Addy was waiting for him in what had to be the most unattractive hiking gear he'd ever seen. She drowned in a pair of baggy, shapeless capri cargo pants that looked like they came from the boy's section of REI.

An oversized t-shirt hung off her petite frame. White socks

poked out from above her beat-up purple hiking boots, and all her hair had been shoved beneath a baseball cap.

"I'm ready," she said with a smile.

"If that's what you call it," he replied under his breath.

Jack packed a quick meal in his own Camelbak and tried not to overthink things.

It's not like she should feel compelled to dress up for me, he reminded himself.

Still, even in that modest getup, he couldn't stop from checking her out as they headed out. Addy started toward the car, but Jack stopped her.

"There's a trail just down the road," he said. "I figured why not explore close to home?"

"Sure," she said with a grin.

Amenable Addy, he thought. *Better than Angry Addy, I guess.*

As they hiked toward the trail he'd noticed on his daily commute, the heat pounded down on them.

"Jesus, it's hot," he said, and wiped his brow.

"I thought it was hotter in Melbourne than here," she teased.

"I think I'm spoiled from all the A/C in the ER."

They hiked in comfortable silence toward the trailhead. Jack noticed Addy as she stole glances at him when she thought he wasn't looking. He suppressed a smile.

She's as hard up as I am, he realized.

That made him feel better, like the score was even.

The trail was blessedly shaded and several degrees cooler. As they reached a flatter area, Jack heard the trickle of a stream.

"Let's follow it," he said.

"Why?"

"Maybe there's a lake nearby."

"There's no lake here, Jack." She was right, but it did lead to a small pool.

"Small blessings," he said as he pulled off his shoes and rolled up his pants.

Addy stared down at him, frozen.

"What, you think I bite?" he asked.

"That's exactly what I'm afraid of." She said it jokingly, but he picked up on the serious undertones.

"C'mon, sit down," he encouraged.

Grudgingly, she made her way beside him and slipped off her own shoes. Addy made sure there was plenty of space between them. Jack pulled out the snacks from his pack along with a bottle of wine.

"We'll have to share the bottle," he said. "I didn't bring any glasses."

"That's fine," she said, too quickly.

Addy inched a little closer to take the bottle, but he could tell she was still guarded.

Jack handed her the bottle, and pointed out the stars on the label.

"Guess which constellation that is," he said. Before she could reply, he filled in the silence. "Leo."

"How do you know?" she asked, genuinely surprised. Finally, the wall she'd put up started to crumble.

"I was obsessed with stars when I was a kid. I thought when I grew up, I'd be an astronaut. That's one goal that will never be reached," he said sadly.

She smiled as she took a swallow of the wine. "I can see that. I bet you were a cute kid."

"The cutest," he corrected. "Hold on, I think I have some photos on my phone."

"Oh my God, you were so freaking cute!" she exclaimed. He watched her expression as she scrolled through the photos. "Ugh, it makes my ovaries hurt to look at you."

"Thanks?" he said with a laugh. "But I was... well, precocious doesn't quite cover it. Looks can be deceiving. What about you? What did you want to be when you were a kid?"

"A horse trainer," she said without hesitation. "Never mind the fact that we couldn't afford a horse. I was determined."

She shook her head at the memory.

"When I was twelve, my parents saved up and bought me a trip to horse camp for a month in the summer. That was the best summer I ever had," she said wistfully. "It was the summer before my mom got sick."

"Ah. Adults getting sick does put a damper on things, doesn't it?"

"Yeah," she said quietly.

He saw her going down a road he wanted desperately to save her from.

"When my dad died, my mom went into a tailspin," he said. "Well, that's a nice way of putting it, actually. She was drunk *all* the time. Pretty much stayed that way ever since."

"Yeah?" Addy asked. Her ears perked up. "Your mom has a... a drinking problem?"

"She's an alcoholic, yes," he said.

"Oh. Is that why you were so good with my dad?"

"Probably," Jack said with a shrug. "I've been dealing with it my whole life, basically."

Addy sat back in silence, an intense expression stretched across her face.

"Can I ask you a question?" Jack asked.

"Sure."

"What are your goals?"

She let out a small laugh. "Is this a career counseling session?"

"I'm just curious."

"Well, taking care of the restaurant, making sure we stay afloat. Taking care of my dad. Making sure Kenzie doesn't get into too much trouble—"

"You're just telling me what you've been doing the past few years. Not that you're not kicking arse at it," he said. "But I mean *your* goals. Those are the goals set by your mom and dad years ago. Tell me what you want to do."

Addy looked at him in surprise. "I don't... I guess I don't know. Nobody's asked me that in so long..."

"Come on," Jack pushed. "I know you've made a list. What's on it?"

"Okay," she said with a blush. "You're right. Well... I want to travel."

"Where?"

"London, Paris, Rome, all the usual places. But also Pondicherry, Istanbul, I want to see the monarch butterfly migration in Mexico. And... I want to fall in love." She said the last part with a shrug, almost like an apology.

"Travel and love," Jack said. "Those are both reasonable."

"Can I have some more wine?" she asked abruptly.

He gazed at her intensely, then purposefully set the wine aside. As he leaned toward her, he watched her blue eyes flutter shut.

It was like touching a flame to tinder. Her mouth opened to his greedily.

Jack couldn't tell if she pulled him on top of her, the plush green clover below them, or if he pushed her down. Either way, as soon as they were on the ground, they started to rip each other's clothes off.

The stiff, too-big shirt she wore came off with ease. The hat came with it and her hair spilled out down her back. She pulled down his pants while he turned her khakis inside out.

Jack lunged for her, desperate to be inside her, but Addy was faster. She went straight for his cock and plunged his length deep into the back of her throat.

He moaned into the forest as she began to work him with an expertise he would have never guessed she possessed. Addy gently cupped his balls.

He looked down at her slender back as she crouched before him. Jack wrapped her long hair around his fist to get a better look of her licking and sucking his hardness. With one hand gripped at his base, the other teased him. She knew exactly how to command his body.

"Fuck," he whispered. "You're going to make me come."

She smiled up at him, her hand still clenched around his base.

"Right here," she said. Addy stuck out her tongue and tapped his tip against it twice. "I want to taste you."

As soon as she took him into the back of her throat again, he exploded inside her. It took all his strength not to grasp her head and stay buried down her throat.

She moaned in pleasure at his taste. The vibration of it milked more out of him than what he thought he had.

Addy wiped her mouth with the back of her hand.

"Did you... did you swallow?" he asked, shocked.

She grinned and felt her jaw. A trickle of his come had run down her lips.

"Well, most of it," she said. She started to search for her clothes to get dressed—but she hadn't wiped all of it from her face.

"Not so fast," he growled.

She squealed as he gripped her thighs and flipped her onto her back. With his thumb, he wiped the wetness from her jaw and spread it across one nipple and the next.

Jack bit her neck and kissed his way down her torso. He flicked her wet nipples with his fingers as he made his way to her mound. Addy spread her legs wider, eager and welcoming.

Jack plunged his tongue into her and she let out a cry. He teased in circles around her clit. She wiggled beneath him, desperate for his lips on her. When he finally did lick and suck at her clit, she writhed in pleasure.

"I'm going to come," she sputtered. "Fuck, I'm close."

She gripped his head and dug her fingers into his hair as she came against his tongue. He felt the gush and lapped up the flood between her thighs.

Gently, he kissed her swollen clit as the waves started to subside. She shivered, but didn't stop him.

"Gentle," she whispered.

"Will you come for me again?" he asked.

Addy moaned in response.

"Come for me again, Addy," he said, and slipped a finger into her.

She gasped. Her body responded with a squeeze to his forefinger. The second time was slower. He could tease her, bring her close to the edge, and back off right before she came.

"Please," she urged finally through gritted teeth.

"Please, what?" he asked with a smile.

Her clit was engorged. He'd managed three fingers inside her and still she pushed up against him, demanding to be fucked with his hand.

"Please let me come," she begged.

He fucked her with his fingers, slow and steady, while his tongue flicked firmly against her clit.

"Oh, Jesus!" she started to cry. "Jack, yes! Jack, I'm coming. I'm coming…"

He felt the pulse against his fingers as she climaxed again. Her cries rang through the forest. She tasted even sweeter the second time around.

When he finally pulled himself up and lay beside her, Addy's eyes were half-closed.

"I needed that," she said as she caught her breath. "But, hey?"

He looked toward her. Addy leaned up on her elbow.

"There are so many reasons it can't ever happen again," she said. "We're on the same page, right?"

"Uh, right," he said, surprised.

But I made you say my name, he thought.

Addy started to get dressed in that ridiculous getup. In a minute, she was fully clothed and had started back toward the trail without him.

18

Addy banged her bare knee against the coffee table, but grit her teeth and continued to scrub furiously at the surface.

There's no way he's going to get to me, she thought.

"You okay?" Jack asked.

He was sprawled across the couch enthralled in the Patriots game on his laptop.

She refused to answer—or give him the satisfaction of rubbing her throbbing knee. Instead, she dropped to all fours and picked up the discarded Red Bull can she'd spotted that morning under the couch.

Men really are pigs, she thought.

Jack crunched into a handful of cashews as she moved to the counter that separated the living room and kitchen. She scrubbed at the gray and white counter aggressively. Some of the sticky streaks were almost impossible to remove.

What the hell is this? she wondered.

Addy figured after years of working in a restaurant, she'd seen and cleaned it all.

"You know, if you're mad, you should just say so," Jack called from the couch.

She whipped her head around and looked at him. His eyes were glued to the screen. He tossed the can of nuts, lid still removed and nowhere in sight, onto the coffee table she'd just cleaned and wiped his salted hand on the couch.

A rage whirled inside her, on the edge of explosion.

"I just cleaned that," she snapped.

"Huh? What?" He glanced at her briefly, but the cheers from the screen pulled his attention back to the game.

"The table? The couch you just wiped your disgusting hand on? I just cleaned that."

Addy slammed the bottle of cleaner on the counter and took the two steps to the couch to stand over him.

"Oh. Sorry, I'll clean it later," he replied.

Yeah, right.

"Hey! You wanted me to talk, I'm talking to you," she said.

"I wanted you to say if you were mad! Not nag me about cleaning. This is my first afternoon off since—well, you know. Calm down."

"Calm down?" She felt the anger that had been whirling inside her start to leak out. "Calm down! Don't freaking tell me to calm down! I'm the only one who cleans this place, and—"

"Nobody asked you to."

"What?" She shook her head in wonder.

"I said nobody asked you to. Forget about it, I'll hire a cleaner," he said with a shrug. "You should relax."

"Hire a…" Addy couldn't believe it.

Everything really was that easy for him, wasn't it?

Not only didn't he care that she'd been the only one cleaning up their place for the past few weeks, it was so easy for him to just replace her just like that.

"Must be nice," she finally said.

"Huh?"

"I said it must be nice! To have money to just throw around like that." She stormed into the kitchen and threw the cleaning supplies into the cabinet.

"Hey!" Jack jumped at the sound. "What, are you pissed again that I can afford a certain lifestyle?"

"You think I'm mad because you have money?" She nearly laughed. *"That's* why you think I'm mad?"

"Well, since you won't tell me why, I have to guess! I was trying to help you out. You seemed pissed off that you 'had' to clean, so I figured—"

"I'm not mad about the cleaning, Jack!" She could hear the trill in her voice, but couldn't stop it. "I'm mad because—oh, never mind."

She stomped into the bedroom as tears threatened to spill down her cheeks.

"What the fuck," she heard him mutter as she slammed the door.

Addy pulled off the shorts that reeked of bleach. Her breath caught when she saw the angry red bruise that had already blossomed on her knee.

That's just great.

Part of her listened for the sound of Jack's footsteps in the hall as she wiggled into jeans and a clean t-shirt, but they never came. Just canned sounds of some ridiculous game drifted in from the living room.

Addy took a deep breath and finger combed her hair out of the topknot.

He's right, she had to admit. *Why the hell are you wasting your time and energy picking up this place, anyway? It's not like it's your real home. Or a real marriage.*

She grabbed her wallet, phone, keys and refused to even look in his direction as she made a beeline for the front door.

"Hey!" Jack said from the couch. "Where are you go—"

Addy slammed the door behind her with a satisfying bang. It cut him off completely and thankfully, she could no longer hear that godawful noise. Her heart rate began to lower as she fired up her little car and headed straight for the closest bar.

"Hi, Addy. Haven't seen you in forever. What'll it be?"

Addy briefly remembered being partnered with the bartender for a science project in middle school.

"Uh," Addy glanced at the time. Just one in the afternoon. "House white, I guess."

She wanted a cocktail, something hard, but the last thing she needed were rumors swirling around town that she was a drunk.

By the time she'd finished half the first glass, the edge—compliments of Jack—had started to soften.

"Long day?" Addy jumped at the voice. When she looked up, Rosalie was beside her. "Mind if I join you?"

Addy shook her head, unable to speak. Rosalie had clearly just come off a grueling shift, but as always she still managed to look perfect.

The staple red lipstick was expertly applied, and the chignon's wisps of escaped hair framed Rosalie's delicate jawline perfectly.

"I'll have the same," Rosalie told the bartender, and gestured at Addy's wine. "So. Jack's off this afternoon. What are you doing at a bar alone?"

Addy began to blush. *Crap. This wasn't going to look good.*

"I just…"

"Needed some alone time?"

Addy gave a soft laugh.

"Something like that." She finished the last of her wine.

"Hold on," Rosalie said. "Is that your first glass?"

"Yeah." *Maybe people will think I'm a drunk even with wine.*

"I need to catch up." In a single swallow, Rosalie downed her entire glass. "Ugh, couldn't you have been drinking liquor or something?"

Addy laughed aloud. The first genuine laugh she'd had in a while, she realized. "I wanted to, but thought that might not look good at one in the afternoon."

"Oh, who cares what anyone thinks?" Rosalie asked. "I just got off a shift from hell, and I'm guessing this is your first afternoon off in a long time. Two shots of Patrón, bartender."

The girl with the jet black hair and full sleeves of tattoos who ran the bar didn't even blink as she poured.

By their second shot, Addy had softened completely. Part of

her couldn't even remember why she'd picked that fight with Jack.

He came from money, she reminded herself. *And what, he's just supposed to start slumming it now that he's with you?*

"So, tell me," Rosalie said.

Even in her buzzed state, she didn't lose that special grace. Her cheeks had turned pinker and her smile was bigger than normal. It gave her a softness that enhanced her beauty even more.

"Tell you what?" Addy asked. She could hear a slight slur in her speech.

That's what you get for drinking on an empty stomach.

"Why you're here alone," Rosalie said. "The real reason, not the PC one."

"Oh." Addy blinked and cradled the little empty shot glass in her hand. "I dunno," she finally said. "I just needed to get away."

Rosalie raised her brows.

"With how much both of you work, I'm surprised you don't take every chance you get to be together. I remember how it was with our sched—sorry, forget I said anything."

"It's okay," Addy said. "I mean, I know you two were together. It's not like pretending otherwise will change that."

"It's still awkward. I get that. I wouldn't be stoked either if I were in your place."

"What do you mean?"

"If my husband worked with his ex all day. Especially the kind of long, odd shifts the hospital requires," Rosalie said with a shrug. "Plus, it's your turf, after all."

Addy laughed. "My turf?"

"You know what I mean," Rosalie said with a laugh. "I mean, this is your hometown. And then you have this whirlwind romance with a new man in town, just to have his ex show up and throw a wrench in the whole thing. It's got telenovela written all over it."

Addy shrugged.

"I'll admit, it was kind of weird at first. The whole thing, not just you," she said quickly. "Trust me, it wasn't in my life plan to marry someone I'd only known for a short amount of time."

More like less than twenty-four hours, she thought.

"The greatest things in life are rarely planned," Rosalie said. "But can I tell you something?"

"Sure."

"Honestly, if Jack had ever looked at me the way he looks at you? Just once? He and I wouldn't have had a problem."

"What's that supposed to mean?"

Part of the alcoholic veil lifted briefly. Addy was aware that this was important, but she couldn't quite find it within herself to surface to soberness.

"It means he's in love with you!" Rosalie said. "It's obvious. With Jack and me, it wasn't ever like that. I mean, I think we both pretended and maybe even hoped one day it would evolve into that—into love—but it just wasn't in the cards."

She shrugged.

Addy laughed.

"You're crazy," she said. "And drunk. And so am I. This probably isn't the best time to be having deep conversations. "

Rosalie shook her head and peered into the empty glass. "You'll see."

19

The stars have aligned.

Jack looked at his phone and smiled at the text from Philip. Ellipses skittered across the screen.

Neither of us are scheduled until Thursday. You and Addy up for an overnight hike? There's a group of us going.

Yes, thank God, he thought.

When Jack had seen the schedule, he knew it was supposed to be a gift. Nobody who worked the ER got two consecutive days off. He should have been grateful, but instead all he could think about was how awkward it would be at home.

Addy was still pissed as hell, and he didn't have a clue why.

Just tell me where to meet and what to bring, he texted back. *Addy can't make it, work.*

Addy's whole "will they or won't they" bullshit was getting out of control. At first, he'd been into her whole angry housewife ploy. And then he realized it wasn't a ploy.

Angry sex was hot, and for a while he'd thought maybe that's what she was into. However, when she'd returned home buzzed from the bar the other afternoon, it was clear she wasn't playing games.

Philip texted him an address downtown and Jack quickly stuffed his camping backpack full of his gear.

This is exactly what you need, he thought as he tossed his tent, bag, and gear into the back of the Jeep. *A night under the stars, a few beers with friends, and a drama-free, Addy-free evening.*

He started to smile as he headed downtown.

Why have I been so stressed out, anyway? he wondered. *So what if Addy's acting crazy? It's not like we're really married.*

Jack bounded into the meeting place, a little diner known for catering to the numerous campers that passed through the area. He stopped short when he saw Rosalie and Addy side by side in a booth.

"What, uh—"

"Hey!" Philip appeared at his side and clapped him on the back. "I thought you said Addy couldn't make it?"

"I didn't think she—"

"She got the day off," Rosalie purred up with a smile.

"She… okay. And what are you…"

"I invited everyone from work," Philip said. "Can you believe all the new kids got two consecutive days off?"

"I invited Addy when I ran into her getting coffee," Rosalie said.

"And I'd just given up my shifts so Dawn could make a little extra. Perfect timing," Addy said with a smile.

But Jack at least knew her well enough to recognize it was forced.

Shit. I can't back out now, he thought. *What were they up to? And since when were Addy and Rosalie friendly?*

"The crew's all here." Jack turned to see Jeremy approach, a backpack slung across his shoulder.

"What—" Jack searched for the words to figure out what the hell was going on, but nothing came out.

"Jeremy! Hi!" One of the nurses that had just started last week jumped up and wrapped her arms around him.

God, does it ever stop? Jack wondered.

Jeremy slung an arm around the girl and surveyed the group.

"This should be fun," he said. His eyes lingered on Jack.

"Let's figure out the car situation. Jack, your Jeep is four-wheel drive, right?"

"Yeah, but I removed the back seats, so there's just room for two."

"My Range Rover is four-wheel drive," Rosalie piped up.

"I'll go with Rosalie to keep her company," Addy said.

"Awesome, okay if I ride with you?" Philip asked Jack.

"Uh, sure."

"Everyone has the address that works with the GPS, right?"

As Jack tore through the town with Philip in the passenger seat, he tried to untangle whatever mess he'd stumbled into. Philip only talked about the trail, the details of his favorite camping site, and gossip from work.

Was he in on it, too? Whatever "it" might be?

The group arrived en masse and everyone immediately started to sort out tents and equipment. Jack had to admit the place was beautiful. Deserted except for them, the lush greenery framed a crystal clear stream seemingly untouched by humans. He could see all the way to the depths.

"Jack!" Philip's voice made him jump.

"Huh, what?"

"I said, how many people does your tent sleep?"

"Oh. Just two." Immediately, he regretted his words. Obviously, he'd be alone with Addy in his tiny tent.

"Oh, alright. You and Addy then, and then I think my tent sleeps…"

He shook his head and went back to staring at the pristine landscape.

"Okay! Everyone ready?" Philip asked. "The hike should just take about an hour round trip, and that'll give us plenty of time to finish setting up the tents when we get back. Jack, you wanna take the lead with me?"

He was grateful at the offer. Addy and Rosalie whispered together in the middle of the pack as the group started toward the trailhead.

What were those two up to?

"Hey," Philip said quietly as they started the incline. "What's up with you and Addy?"

Shit.

"Marital woes," Jack finally said. "No biggie, though."

"You want to talk about it?" Philip asked. He glanced behind them, but Addy and Rosalie were in their own world yards behind them, chattering like schoolgirls. "If I can help—"

"I said it's no big deal," Jack said. "Can we just enjoy the trail?"

Philip clamped his mouth shut. Five minutes later, he started to talk about work, and Jack settled into the safe subject, thankful to forget about Addy for a few hours.

By the time they circled back to the campsite, Jack had almost forgotten that Addy—not to mention Rosalie and Jeremy—were right behind them.

The brief but challenging hike had given the adrenaline junkie in him a little high. When he saw Addy's tanned legs before him as he hunkered down over the little tent, he looked up with a smile on his face.

To his surprise, it seemed like the fight in her had been drained.

"Can I help?" she asked.

He glanced around to see if someone was nearby, if there was a show they needed to be putting on. But everybody else was busy setting up their own tents.

"I've got it, but thanks," he said.

"Yeah," she said quietly. "You've got it all figured out by yourself."

His eyes shot upward. She acted like nothing had happened between them, but now he recognized that simmer below her surface.

"Maybe, uh, maybe we should set this up a little over here," he said, and pulled the tent away from the main group.

"Oh, someone needs some privacy!" one of his coworkers called out. He ignored the kissing noises that came their way.

Great, he thought.

By the time everyone had their tents set up and their

equipment put away, it was dark. Philip had built a roaring fire in the pit, and the group had assembled a circle of chairs around the flames that licked dangerously toward the sky.

"Cheers!" Rosalie said as she opened a bottle of wine and everyone filled their red Solo cups with a sweet red.

After just one drink each, everyone who worked at the hospital began to yawn.

Wow. We really are lame, Jack thought.

"You guys," Rosalie said. "I hate to be that person, but I'm exhausted."

"Seriously?" Jeremy asked. He shook his head in disgust and pulled out a silver flask.

"I'm pretty tired, too," said the nurse who'd brought Jeremy.

He shot her a look of disappointment, but said nothing.

"I think it's safe to say most of us are beat," Philip said. "I don't have a problem calling it a night and getting an early start on another hike in the morning. I mean, we came out here to relax, right?"

Out of the corner of his eye, Jack watched Addy trace a design into the dirt with a long stick. She shot a look of daggers at Philip.

Wow. She really doesn't want to be stuck in that tent with me, Jack thought.

It was going to be a long night. He prayed that the glass of wine would do its trick and just put him to sleep.

As Philip doused the fire and the group began to disperse to their tents, Addy shot toward theirs at lightning speed.

"Someone's eager," Philip said quietly and nudged Jack with his elbow.

If he only knew.

Addy had left the entry flap open and was already curled up in her sleeping bag. Jack opened the flashlight app on his phone and made his way into the cramped tent.

He slipped out of his jeans and t-shirt, bundling them into the corner. Addy faced away from him.

As Jack slipped into his own sleeping bag in boxers, he let out a sigh. It looked like she'd just ignore him the entire night, which was fine with him.

"Do you mind?" she hissed.

"What?"

"You didn't bring any pajamas? You're just going to sleep naked—"

"How do you even know—Jesus, Addy, I'm wearing boxers!"

"Keep your voice down!" She flipped over as his eyes adjusted to the darkness.

Overhead, he'd kept the flap off the top of the tent to let the stars shine through. The moon was bright enough that it dimly illuminated their tent. Addy glared at him and squinted as her own eyes adapted.

"What's your problem?" he asked, incredulous.

"You're my problem," she growled.

He opened his mouth to argue, but something about her in that blue light made him stop. Jack lunged for her. Her lips were soft and tasted wild, yet familiar.

Addy made a small squeak and weakly pushed him away. It just made him want her more. When he kissed her a second time, there was no resistance. Instead, she parted her lips and welcomed his tongue against hers.

"Addy—"

"Shut up." She rose to her knees and the sleeping bag fell away from her. In one swift motion, she pulled off her t-shirt to reveal full breasts with hard nipples that begged for his mouth.

20

She hated herself for it, but she just couldn't stop.

The feel of his mouth against hers, his tongue as it flicked across her teeth, it was all too much.

Addy scrambled out of her sleeping bag and Jack reached for the little shorts. He tore them off with ease. When Addy reached for her underwear to pull them down, he grabbed her wrists and stopped her.

Jack pushed her against the thin material of the tent, grasped her ankles and spread her legs wide. As he crawled toward her, hand still on her ankles, she whimpered.

In nothing but panties, which were quickly becoming soaked, goosebumps broke out across her flesh and her nipples grew harder. Jack nuzzled into her neck and began to trail his tongue down her collarbone.

As he moved downward, she pushed her chest out, desperate for his mouth on her nipples. He kissed her breasts and outlined her areolas with the tip of his tongue.

Jack teased her and she moaned in frustration. Finally, when he pulled a nipple into his mouth and started to suck, Addy cried out.

Jack worked toward her other breast and she wound her fingers through his hair. He kissed down her stomach. Addy started to pant as he neared the hemline of her panties.

He kissed her clit through the lacy material and she moaned, on the edge of explosion already. When she looked down at the sight of his head between her legs, his big hands wrapped tight around her ankles, it was almost too much to bear.

"Please," she whispered.

"Please, what?" he asked, but he didn't look at her. "Tell me what you want."

"Come on," she said. As much as she didn't want to, she pushed her center toward his face.

"Tell me what you want," he repeated.

What do you want? Emboldened, she gripped his hair tighter.

"Rip my panties off," she said.

He released her ankles just long enough to oblige. The chill in the air instantly hit the warm wetness of her center.

"Now?" he asked.

"Eat me."

"Eat what?" he asked, and blew lightly on her clit.

"Eat my pussy." The voice didn't sound like her, low and hungry.

Immediately, Jack's tongue was on her clit. Without the buffer of the lace between his tongue and her, the pleasure hit hard. She closed her eyes and lifted her head upward.

"What else do you want?" he asked between kisses and sucks.

"Put your finger in me," she demanded.

Addy didn't even realize that's what she wanted, to feel only partially full of him, until she said it. He released one ankle and easily slid a thick finger through her wetness. She moaned and pressed against it, but needed more.

"Two fingers," she said.

Addy opened her eyes and she looked down at Jack, so eager to please her. The power of it, of telling him exactly how to fuck her, was intoxicating. She started to play with her breasts, to pinch her nipples.

But why should I have to?

"Here," she said, and took his hand that still gripped an ankle and brought it to her breasts. Eagerly, he started to roll one nipple in his finger. It inched her closer to orgasm.

"Yes," she said, and spread her legs wider. Every part of him was for her pleasure. "My G-spot," she said, her voice shaking. "Hit my G-spot."

Jack's fingers inside her changed rhythm and position. In seconds, she felt the waves he commanded inside her start to move.

As she got close to orgasm, she forced herself to stop—and Jack.

"Slower," she managed to say. "Slow down." He obliged, but even she could tell how difficult it was for him. "Give me your hand."

Jack slowly slid his fingers from her center.

"Let me taste," she demanded.

He raised his hands to her lips while his tongue lazily circled her engorged clit. As she sucked his fingers, slick with her wetness, to the depths of her throat she heard a feral purr deep inside her.

"Do you want to fuck me?" she asked as she released his fingers from her lips.

"Yes," he said from between her thighs.

She squeezed her legs together, trapped his head between them. "How badly do you want to fuck me?"

"More than anything."

"From behind."

As soon as she'd spoken the words, he was on his knees and tore off his boxers. Addy bit her lip and admired his swollen cock.

She got onto all fours and smiled at him from over her shoulder.

"Fuck me now," she said lowly.

Jack gripped her hips and buried himself deep inside with a groan.

"Oh, fuck," she whispered.

His length pressed hard against her G-spot and her clit began to throb. As he began his rhythm, she squirmed.

"Wait," she said, and he stopped immediately. The power was incredible. "Like this."

Addy raised onto her knees, perched on top of his thighs with his cock deep within her. At this angle, the pressure against her G-spot was almost too much to take. Jack kissed her neck from behind.

"Harder," she said, and he bit down just enough to make her yelp. One of his hands reached for her clit and the other ran across her breasts.

"Just like that," she said.

Jack started to bounce her while he stimulated every sensual part of her body.

She could feel his breath, ragged, against her ear as he sucked the delicate skin of her neck.

"Addy," he whispered into her ear. "Fuck, you feel so good."

"Make me come," she said, though she was already close. He began to fuck her harder.

"Make me come," she said again, louder with her head dropped back.

"I'm close," he said, almost apologetic.

What the hell? No condom. Fuck, there was no condom.

But in that moment, she didn't care.

"Make me come with you," she said. "Come inside me."

"Addy—"

"Come inside me."

With a final flick of his slick finger against her clit, he nipped at her neck and slammed her down onto him.

"Fuck, Jack," she cried out, and clenched her teeth together.

The rush of his come exploded inside her and pushed her over the edge. She called out his name and came hard against his cock.

He released her and Addy fell forward onto her hands and knees, but he stayed inside her. His hands once again at her hips, he pulled her close.

"Let me feel you," she heard him say from behind. "I want to feel it…"

"Again," she whispered. "Just a little… fuck, Jack, I'm going to come again."

She'd barely come off the first wave, but the rush of his

orgasm inside her brought on an entire new climax. She pushed her ass against him and mewled through the second round.

When he finally released her and pulled himself out, she felt a hot stream of their combined juices spill out of her. The wetness ran down her leg.

Addy turned around to find him splayed on his back, one arm outstretched for her to fall against his chest.

But Addy stayed as far away as she could in the cramped tent and hurriedly pulled on her t-shirt.

"What's wrong?" he asked.

"Nothing," she said, impressed that she was able to muster her professional voice. She searched for her shorts but couldn't find them in the tangled mess of sleeping bags.

"Shit," she said. "Move, I can't find my shorts."

"Addy, don't worry about it," he said. "Come here—"

"No," she snapped. Even in the low light, she could see the cloud move across his face.

"What's your problem?"

"Nothing," she said. "Actually, that's not true. You're my problem."

"Excuse me?"

"You're a fucking bad life choice for me, Jack!" she said.

"Well, thanks a lot."

"That's not what I meant."

She finally found the shorts and pulled them up, not caring that both of their come continued to seep out of her and directly onto the material.

"Okay, then what did you mean?"

"I mean this wasn't supposed to happen! This whole thing, it was a stupid fucking mistake to begin with. Fine, okay? I own part of that, we were both shitfaced drunk when we got married. But we *stayed* married to get back at Rosa—"

"Addy! Shh," he said, and leaned up on his elbows.

She glanced toward the entry flap and remembered about Rosalie and Jeremy just a few yards away.

"Sorry," she said, her voice lower. "But ... God, Jack, don't you get it?"

"Apparently not."

"I was okay faking a marriage that we'd already stupidly put ourselves into anyway. Or, at least as okay as I could be."

"So what changed?"

"*This*," Addy gestured to the space between them. "This wasn't supposed to happen."

"I thought you liked it."

"That's not the point!"

"Why not?" He looked at her, wholly confused.

"I mean… I'm starting to *feel* things, Jack. Okay? Things that… I shouldn't be feeling since the whole thing is fake. I—"

"You mean you like me?"

"Yeah, okay, whatever you want to call it. And this… all this sex, it isn't helping."

"Is this because of the no condom thing? I thought you were on the pill or something. If not, I mean we can get the morning-after pill. We'll go right now if you want."

"Jesus, Jack, yes, I'm on the pill, okay? That's not, fuck, that's not what I'm worried about."

"Then what are you worried about?"

I'm worried that I'm falling in love with you. That I'm already way too deep into this. That you're going to break my heart. That you coming inside me is going to make it even worse.

I'm worried that I can't stop.

"Nothing," she said. "Forget it."

21

The drive back to their condo was clouded with such strong sexual tension Jack didn't know if he could stand it.

Part of him wanted to pull over on the side of the road and take her again like that—wild and unrestrained where every car that passed by could see. But he held it together.

Thank God the next morning's hike was short and that both Rosalie and Jeremy behaved.

He was so goddamned distracted by Addy that he didn't know how he'd managed to function.

He glanced over at her as they took the exit toward their condo. Jack couldn't read her expression behind her sunglasses as she gazed into the distance. He traced the outline of her body with his eyes.

There was the slightest gap in the buttons of her flannel shirt, and he thought he could see a snippet of the flesh beneath. Her shorts were hiked up to the swell of her thighs.

He wanted to reach over and squeeze her leg, but there was no telling how she would react.

Last night had been incredible, how she'd taken charge like that. At the same time, he knew the power was his. She might have been giving the orders, but he was the one who'd made her respond like that. Who'd made her come, made her call out his name and demand more.

He hardened just at the memory of it.

In the morning, Addy had sheepishly asked Philip about showers.

"Showers?" Philip had nearly laughed. "This isn't glamping! It's just an overnight trip, but if you're really hurting for one you can always take a dip in the stream. It's probably near freezing though, mountain runoff."

Addy had seriously looked at that freezing cold water for a minute. Jack had come up behind her and wrapped his arms around her waist—he knew she couldn't push him away since everybody else was up, about, and may be watching.

"No showers," he'd whispered in her ear. "I want you to smell like me all day."

She'd stiffened in his arms, but resisted the urge to force his arms away.

As soon as he parked the car, she jumped out of the Jeep and headed straight for the door. Jack paused, one arm already stretched out to unpack the car, but he changed his mind. He was right behind her and flung the door open almost as soon as it shut.

Addy jumped at the sound and turned to face him.

"What do you want?" she asked and crossed her arms across her chest.

"You know what I want."

"No," she said, and shook her head. "Jack—"

He closed the distance between them with ease and grabbed the bottom of her shirt. With a tug, the pearl snap buttons of her shirt flew open to reveal her bare breasts. Addy gasped into his mouth, but didn't resist.

"No bra, huh?" he said as he traced his tongue from her mouth to her jaw. "Looks like this is just what you wanted."

"No, I—"

"Shh," he said.

With ease, he hoisted her up until her breasts were at his face. Addy's hands rested on his shoulders as he took one of those perfect nipples between his lips and sucked. He felt the toe of her hiking boot brush lightly against his thigh.

"This is what I like about you," he said as he kissed his way to her other breast. The open material of her flannel flicked against his face. "You're funsized."

As he lowered her, he kissed his way up her neck to her lips. When he'd returned her feet to the floor, her head remained upturned, hungry for more.

"Take off your shorts."

She began to slide the shirt off her shoulders first.

"No, just the shorts. Keep the shirt and boots on. And take off your panties—if you're wearing any."

She looked at him slightly curiously, but followed his directions. Jack wasn't surprised to see that she wore nothing under the shorts. He sat down on the couch and pulled her close.

The lips of her labia were already puffy. Jack pulled her toward him and kissed her stomach as his fingers explored between her thighs. She was sticky, sweet, and ready just like always.

"Look at this," he said, and he showed her how wet his fingers were.

Slowly, he separated his thumb and middle finger. Her viscous wetness clung between his fingers, creating a thread.

Addy blushed and tucked her hair behind her ears.

Where was the confident girl from last night?

"Here," he said, and lay down on the couch. Jack put his head on the armrest. "Sit," he said, and gestured to his face. "Right here."

"Jack, I—"

"Sit."

Just like in his dream, she straddled his mouth and faced away from him. She was so petite there was no more than an inch of space between her wetness and his mouth.

Still, she held back. Addy didn't lower herself, so Jack closed their distance by darting his tongue into her center. That was all it took.

Addy shuddered and let out a moan as she lowered onto his

face. She readjusted herself, leaned forward slightly and directed her clit onto his tongue.

Jack gripped her ass as Addy leaned her hands on her thighs and began to ride his face. She was in complete control, and her ass wiggled wildly in his hands. He watched her tits bounce overhead, nipples hard, while Addy occasionally pinched and pulled at them.

She was fucking gorgeous, eyes closed as she rode his face, with her only thought on the sheer pleasure he gave her.

When she shifted and offered up her opening, he dove his tongue as deeply inside her as he could and delighted in the taste of her. As he fucked her with his tongue, she groaned and bounced against his mouth.

He could still taste last night on her, their combined sweat and traces of his own come. Jack gripped her ass tighter. His tongue made its way to the rim of her ass.

She cried out his name as he circled the tight bud of her opening.

Addy leaned forward and presented her clit to him once again.

"I'm almost there," she said. "Jack, I'm –"

"Come on my face," he said. He barely got the words out before a gush rushed onto his tongue.

"Jack!" she cried out. "Jack…"

"You taste so good," he said, his hands wrapped around her thighs to keep her close.

He could have lapped her up all day, the taste was almost addictive.

She moaned and settled onto his face, the grinding slow. "What about you…" she said sleepily.

"Don't worry about me, I'm fine," he said.

Addy stood up.

"No," she said. "Let me take care of you. What do you want?" she asked.

Addy bent down and ran her hand along the hardness below his pants.

"Get on top," he said, and rushed to unbuckle his belt.

Anything, he would have given *anything* to make his dream come true, and now it was.

Addy smiled when his cock sprung out of his pants. The flannel shirt had slipped nearly off and bunched at her elbows.

"Ride me," he said.

The ache was almost unbearable. Addy straddled him, took his cock and ran her thumb along the tip, slick with precum. She furrowed her brow as she guided him in, still sensitive.

"Fuck, you feel good," he said. She smiled at him, and he grabbed her waist and pushed her down. She cried out when he filled her up.

"Stay," he said. "Just stay like this a minute."

Jack was completely inside her and every instinct within him told him to move. To bounce her, to fuck her, to fill her with his come. But this, this closeness, it overrode everything else.

He watched her sensitivity vanish. Addy put her hands on his chest and began to writhe. Her boots dug into the sides of his legs. Addy technically did as he said.

She didn't ride the length of his cock, but he could tell by her squirms that she was hitting her G-spot with his hardness as best she could.

"You want to fuck me?" he asked.

She looked him in the eye and nodded.

"Are you going to come for me again?"

"Yes," she said, almost breathless.

She continued to press against him, harder and more demanding. Jack was ready to explode. He knew he wouldn't last long this time. He needed her too badly.

"Addy... how bad do you want it?"

"More than anything," she said, echoing his words with a smile.

"Ask nicely," he said as he ran his fingers up her thighs and made her shiver.

"Please let me fuck you," she said.

Her fingernails dug into his chest and her eyes rolled back in her head.

"Are you going to fuck me right, like a good wife?" he asked.

She paused, but only for a second. "Yes."

"Say it, then."

"I'm going to fuck you like a good wife," she said. Her wetness leaked down his hips. "Come on..."

"Say it one more time," he said. With all his strength, he pressed her down hard onto him.

"You're my husband," she moaned. "And I'll fuck you right, like a good wife."

"Go on then."

He released her hips and Addy went wild. Her yelps punctuated her thrusts as she rode him and rubbed her clit against his taut stomach.

Just as he felt himself release inside her, she let out that now-familiar cry of her own orgasm.

"So good," she whispered, over and over. "Jack, it feels so good."

She stayed on top of him until every last wave of her orgasm faded. He felt his own come start to slip out of her and bind them together.

This time, when she released him from her center, she didn't immediately look for her clothes.

Addy fell, almost asleep already, readily into his arms and nuzzled her cheek against his chest.

22

"Come on, Grandma," Kenzie said as she bolted past Addy in the kitchen. "What's wrong with you today? This is the first time, like, ever that I'm actually faster than you at work."

"Sorry," Addy mumbled as she balanced the plates on her forearm.

The last thing she was going to do was tell Kenzie she could barely walk because of yesterday's session on the couch with Jack. She didn't know what had come over her—or him.

What had happened in the tent was one thing. It was fueled by passion, anger, and the sheer strangeness of being in close quarters in the wild. But at home? She still couldn't unravel that one. Worse, she wanted to do it again.

Addy considered pulling a double shift today a blessing. At least Jack couldn't distract her.

Or could he? she wondered.

"Addy." She almost dropped the plates she held as she served them to the customers at table nine.

"Dawn," she gave a fake smile over her shoulder. "What's up?"

The customers dug into their meals and ignored the two waitresses completely.

"Can I talk to you a minute?"

Addy rolled her eyes at Dawn's back as she followed the towering bleached blonde to the kitchen.

God, Dawn acts like she's the manager.

"What's so important that you made me almost spill meatloaf on a customer?" she asked.

"The hospital called."

"Jack?" She was confused. Why wouldn't he just text her?

"No, I mean, the hospital—I don't know who it was. Your dad just got admitted—"

"Shit." Addy immediately started toward the little cage of lockers for her purse. "Is he okay? What happened?"

She could have kicked herself for that last question.

Alcohol, that's what happened.

"They said he's stable," Dawn called after her. "But it sounds like he called 9-1-1. An ambulance took him—"

"Can you cover for me?" she asked. "Shit. And Kenzie?"

"What? I mean, I guess. I'll have to call in one of the new girls—"

"Thanks," Addy said, and shot her a smile. She nearly ran right into Kenzie as she ran toward the exit.

"Not that fast!" Kenzie said. "God, Addy, you almost hit me."

"Come on, Dad's in the hospital." Without a word, Kenzie tossed the tray of dirty dishes she had onto the counter.

"Hey!" Dawn called, but neither of them turned back.

Kenzie chewed at her cuticle madly in the passenger seat as Addy raced toward the hospital.

"Do you think he'll be okay? Addy, do you think he'll be okay?"

"I don't know, stop asking," Addy snapped. Guilty, she stole a look at Kenzie, who had chewed her nail until it bled.

"I'm sure he'll be fine," she said softly. "Probably just needs his stomach pumped or something."

Kenzie looked uncertain, but she grew quiet.

By some miracle, there was a spot directly in front. Kenzie kept pace with her as they flew into the ER.

"Mrs. Stratton!" the receptionist called in greeting. "Are you here for Ja—"

With wild eyes, Addy went straight for her.

"Ted Fuller," she said, out of breath.

"What?"

"Ted Fuller."

"Where's our dad?" Kenzie yelled at the woman.

"Oh! Uh—" the receptionist's hands flew across the keyboard. "Theodore Fuller has been moved to the ICU. That's your fath—"

"Thanks," Addy said. She grabbed Kenzie's hand and ran toward the ICU wing. She saw Jack as he paced back and forth beside the check-in desk. "Jack! What happened? Where is he—"

"It's okay," Jack said. He grabbed her shoulders as she approached him and steadied her. "He's... he's alright."

"He's okay?" Kenzie asked. Her voice trembled.

"What happened?" Addy demanded. "Where is he?"

"It's his heart," Jack said slowly.

"His heart? He... he didn't get his stomach pumped? He wasn't drunk?"

"He... well, he was," Jack said carefully. "Sometimes excessive amounts of alcohol can raise the blood pressure to such a degree that it can lead to a heart attack—"

"Oh, God, he had a heart attack?" Kenzie cried. "It's my fault. I should have... I should have..."

"There's nothing either of you could have done. This was caused by years of heavy drinking, coupled with excess weight and maybe even a history of high blood pressure. We're still waiting on the files from his GP to confirm that."

"So what... what now?" Addy asked, her eyes filled with tears.

"Now we wait," Jack said. "There's nothing to be done except keep him overnight to be monitored."

"Can we see him?" Kenzie asked.

"No, I'm afraid not. Besides, he's been sedated and will be asleep until tomorrow anyway," Jack said. "Try not to worry, that won't help anything."

"Easy for you to say," Kenzie muttered.

Addy elbowed her.

"Dr. Stratton? We need you in here," a nurse said crisply as she walked by.

"Hold on a minute, I'll be right back."

Addy sank into a hard plastic chair beside Kenzie and held her sister's hand.

"It'll be okay," she said.

"It's all my fault," Kenzie repeated under her breath.

"No," Addy said, though she knew there was nothing she could say to make Kenzie believe her.

"Addy? Kenzie?" Jack returned at a fast clip. "I'm totally slammed today, but listen. I've read your father's chart and I'm keeping an eye on him, along with the rest of his team. I promise you, he'll be fine. There's nothing to worry about. But you won't be able to see him until tomorrow at the earliest, so there's no reason for you to stick around here."

"I have to stay," Kenzie said stubbornly.

"No, let's go back to the house," Addy said. She glanced at Jack. "Get it nice and cleaned up before he gets home."

Kenzie looked from Addy to Jack. "But what if he wakes up—"

"There's no way, not with the sedatives he's on," Jack said. "I promise you, nothing will happen. I'm on shift here for another five hours. I give you my word."

AT THE HOUSE, Addy wrinkled her nose at the smell. It hit her as soon as she walked through the doors, but Kenzie seemed immune. It was easy enough to find the main source.

Nobody had emptied the garbage or recycling for at least two weeks. Addy wanted to complain, to ask Kenzie how she could live like this. But whenever she looked at her sister with that quivering lip, she stopped herself.

Side by side, they cleaned each room. For once, Kenzie didn't hesitate or complain. She did exactly as Addy said, happy to take directions.

Just as they finished up, Addy's phone buzzed while she put away the mop.

He's OK, Jack texted. *Come home.*

Addy blinked, surprised.

Had it already been five hours? she thought.

She didn't want to leave Kenzie, but as soon as Kenzie realized the cleaning was over she turned on the television and seemed to forget Addy existed.

"Are you going to be okay here?" she asked Kenzie.

"Yeah," Kenzie sank into the couch and flipped on *The Great British Bake Off.* "I just need to zone out."

"If you're sure. Do you want me to stay?"

Kenzie didn't reply.

"Okay…" Addy said. "I guess I'll go home then. Call me if you need me?"

Kenzie nodded, transfixed by the cherries jubilee being crafted on the screen.

"I'll check in with you before I go to bed," Addy said. "And we'll go to the hospital first thing in the morning. I'll text you when I head over."

"Okay," Kenzie called behind her.

On the short drive to Jack's condo, to their condo, Addy tried not to think about worst case scenarios. *What if… what if… what if…*

She was close to tears by the time she parked next to Jack's Jeep and trudged inside. What had happened to Kenzie? It was like she turned into a zombie as soon as they'd finished cleaning. Was it just her way of dealing?

"How are you?" Jack asked when she walked in.

He'd just emerged from the bathroom, and his large frame filled the doorway to the hall.

She opened her mouth to reply, but nothing came out. Addy fell into his arms.

"Hey, it's okay," he whispered to her. "It's going to be okay."

She tilted her head up to see his eyes, to gauge if he was being truthful, but the hunger she saw in them overwhelmed her.

"Take me to bed," she said, her voice strong and steady.

"Addy, I don't know—"

"Don't you want me?" she asked.

The throb had started between her legs. She needed him to make her forget, to make her feel whole again.

Addy took a step back and slowly unbuttoned her white work shirt. She maintained eye contact as she unhooked her bra.

Jack let out a growl and pulled her close. As he explored her mouth with his tongue, he walked backward to the bed. She felt his hardness press against her lower abdomen as his hands hitched up her black skirt.

Addy sat on the bed and pulled down his scrubs. She licked her lips and bent forward for his cock, but he pushed her down on the bed and climbed on top of her, too eager for her to finish undressing either of them.

As Jack plunged into her, she squeezed her eyes shut and gasped. He felt so good, the way he filled her completely. It took her somewhere else entirely.

"Slow," she whispered. "Fuck me slow. I want to feel it."

He buried his face in her neck and kissed her gently. His lips roamed across the hickeys he'd peppered on her skin the past few days.

She delighted in every inch he gave her, at the pressure that lingered when he pressed against her clit. Each time he was at his deepest, she clutched at his back and held him closer.

The slowness of it, the intensity, brought her quickly to orgasm.

"You're making me come," she choked out.

"Yes, come for me. Come for me, Addy," he encouraged into her ear.

She trembled against the waves as he came with her and filled her with the heat she so desperately needed.

23

"Dr. Stratton, there's a call for you," Nurse Bostian said.

"For me? Who is it?"

"I don't know, I'm a nurse, not a receptionist."

Jack stalked toward the front desk. He couldn't be cross with the nurse. It was highly frowned upon to get personal calls at the hospital, but not against the rules. *Who the hell would call the hospital and not my phone?* "Hello?"

"Jacob, it's me." His mom's Melbourne accent was crystal clear across the lines.

"Mum? Why didn't you call my phone?"

"I did, you didn't answer your phone," she sniffed.

"Right, because I'm at work. You know, in the ER."

"Surely you can get away for a few minutes. As you just did."

"The, uh... the connection is pretty good."

"That's because I'll be landing there in an hour."

"Here? Tahoe? In an hour?"

"Jacob, that's what I just said. You need to listen better."

"It's just that... well, it's quite a surprise."

"I asked when your shift was up, and it's any minute now, correct?"

"Yes..."

"So shall we say dinner at six o'clock? That should give you time to freshen up. I trust that you know the decent restaurants in town by now."

"I do, but—"

"Fantastic, I'll give you a call when I land. Do answer your phone this time, won't you, Jacob?"

"Yes, Mum," he muttered.

"Sounded urgent," the receptionist said and gave him a sideways look.

"Highly."

Jack looked at the clock. He was off in ten minutes, assuming there were no urgent cases that came in. He started toward his locker and tried to piece together how this would go. Surprisingly, the first person he wanted to reach out to was Addy.

Or maybe that's not so surprising anymore.

When he grabbed his phone from the charging station, he saw that there was indeed a missed call from an unknown number. He took a deep breath and called Addy's phone.

"What's up?" she asked. She sounded breathless. "I'm just on a run to the bank for more change."

"What time are you off?"

"Uh, about an hour. Why?"

"My mum's come to town."

"What?"

"And she's a picky bitch."

"Jack!"

"Sorry, love, but there's no time for tact. We're having dinner at six."

"We are?"

"Yeah, is that enough time for you to get ready after work?"

"I mean... I guess? I could have used more warning—"

"Same here. Oh, and one more thing? She might not know that I'm married, per se."

"Excuse me? What the—then why the hell do I even need to go? This is going way past what we agreed upon—"

"That's what I love about you, how you roll with the punches."

Dr. Hottie 151

"Jack, I'm serious."

"Look, I'm sorry. She took me by surprise, too. But do this for me, and I swear I'll make it up to you. I'll shelter you from her as much as I can, too."

"Oh my—fine. Whatever. Where are we going?"

"Same place we had that incredible triple date before. Only the best for Mum."

Addy groaned.

"Can I meet you there? I don't have anything clean to wear, I need to raid Kenzie's closet. And check on Dad," she added.

Jack gulped. He felt guilty about springing this on Addy when her dad had only been home from the hospital for just three days.

"Yeah, sure, love. Meet us there."

———

JACK WAITED on the tarmac for his mother's plane. It wasn't unusual for private planes to land in Tahoe, but he still felt like he was getting stares from the locals who worked there.

He tried to shake it off, but it still got to him. He'd hoped to leave the spoiled rich kid shadow behind. But as soon as his mother was en route, it all came back.

When her plane arrived, the ground crew immediately hustled toward the private jet. She emerged with newly shorn hair, a razor-sharp silver bob that had been her signature look for as long as Jack could remember.

Her cream silk skirt suit was impeccably tailored, without a wrinkle in sight. She didn't even bother to remove her Jackie O sunglasses as she swished toward Jack, used to everyone rolling out the red carpet treatment for her.

"Jacob," she said, and air kissed both his cheeks.

"It's Jack," he said, but she brushed it off as always.

She finally did remove her glasses to take in the Jeep as he hoisted her Louis Vuitton Damier luggage in the back.

"Mum?" he asked, as held the door open for her.

"I'm not getting in your trashy little plaything, darling," she said, her nose wrinkled. "Fortunately, I know how boys are. Even ones raised to such high standards. It's a good thing I had my assistant order a chauffeured town car. Where's the transportation entrance? They said they'd wait there."

He gritted his teeth and escorted her to the sleek black town car.

"Oh, just come with me, darling," she said. "Nobody's about to steal that tank of yours."

"Where to?" he asked as he slid in beside her.

Jack knew better than to suggest she stay with him, at a hotel, or anywhere else. She was a force to be reckoned with, and it was always better to let her take the lead.

"The hospital," she said as she pulled out a compact to check her makeup.

"The... my hospital?"

"Oh, you hardly own it. The one you *work* at, dear," she said. "I thought we'd do that first, so I could see how you spend your days. Doesn't that sound nice?"

He felt his heart rate increase the closer they got to the hospital.

"Just wait right here," she told the driver.

"Mum, this is for ambulances," Jack tried.

"Well, I'm certain he's capable of *moving* temporarily should one arrive," she said.

Even in her teetering stilettos, she managed to stay a few paces ahead of him.

He was greeted with surprised and confused looks from the rest of the staff. "I thought you were off for the night," Philip said.

"I am—I was. This is my mum, Diana."

"Mrs. Stratton," she corrected.

Philip held out a hand and offered up his winning grin, but she paused uncomfortably long.

"I'm sorry, dear," she told Philip. "Don't take it personally, but considering the place and your job, I don't know where those hands have been."

"Oh! Right, okay," Philip said.

He gave Jack an odd look as he pretended to look at his pager and wandered off.

Jack felt the shame thicken around him as his mother was rude to everyone they approached—until she caught sight of Rosalie.

"Rosalie, darling!" she called.

Rosalie whipped around. It took her a moment to recognize Diana, but when everything clicked into place Jack saw Rosalie freeze. He easily remembered their last, and only meeting—it had been just a brief dinner, but his mum had been cold and frosty to her.

What's she up to?

"Mrs. Stratton," Rosalie said. "What a surprise."

She accepted the air kisses, but shot Jack a *What the hell?* look over his mother's shoulder.

"Well, when I found out that you followed my Jacob here, I realized just how serious you two were."

"Excuse me? I didn't follow—"

"Mum!"

"Oh, hush," she said, and patted Jack's hand. "Rosalie, dear, you must join us for dinner."

"Dinner?" Rosalie looked at Jack, confused.

"Mum, I'm sure Rosalie will still be on shift—"

"What time are you done, dear?"

"Uh, in about thirty—"

"Perfect, we'll see you there. Jacob? I'm ready to leave," his mother said.

"Alright. We'll text you the details," he muttered, happy to get her out of there as quickly as possible.

Before they'd even exited, she began to pick apart the building.

"Poor quality craftsmanship is all I can say," she said. "Honestly, Jacob, I don't understand why you would leave your prospects in Melbourne for… this."

Jack was quiet. She egged him on, but there was no way he'd let her rile him up before she met Addy.

"Where to?" the driver asked after he'd opened their door and slid back into the front seat.

Jack looked to his mother, who raised her brow.

"Well?" she asked. "Give him your address, Jacob."

Shit. No hotel? He mumbled the address to the driver. Jack could feel his mother's appraisal of him as they made the short drive.

"Haven't had time for the gym lately," his mother said. It was a statement, not a question.

"Been busy," he said.

"Too busy to even get out into the sun? That's the one good thing about this place in the summer. You look sickly without a tan, Jacob."

"Yeah, well. I'm a doctor, Mum. Kind of busy."

"Jacob, don't make excuses. If your father could do it, so can you."

He clenched his fist and jaw, but the buzz of his phone distracted him.

Just got back to the condo, Addy said. *Got a black dress from Kenzie that I think will work.*

"Here we are," the driver said as he pulled up to the building.

Jack's mother peered at the craftsman-style condos and raised one judgmental brow. "Jacob—"

"Mum, I need you to listen to me."

The driver got out of the car and came toward their door.

"It's very important that you be nice to the person you're about to meet."

"About to mee—Jacob." She scowled. "I knew it. You moved here for a girl, didn't you—"

"I met her after I moved here," he said, cutting her off.

The driver opened the door and offered an arm to his mother. She took it with a huff.

"Be nice," he repeated as he opened the door.

"I'm *always* nice, Jacob."

Addy sprung off the couch as soon as he threw open the door. Jack saw that she'd madly cleaned the condo as best she could. Even in the crazed state only his mother could put him in, he couldn't help but notice how incredible Addy looked.

Her hair was blown out and the black dress with the lace cap sleeves hugged her figure perfectly but balanced modesty and sensuality.

"Addy, this is my mum, Diana. Mum, this is my wife, Addison. Addy."

Addy reached out her hand. He saw the usual disgust in his mother's face, but it faltered at the word "wife."

"I'm so happy to finally meet you, Mrs. Stratton," Addy said.

"Your... your..." his mother said. He'd never seen her shaken like this before.

Before Addy could realize his mother wouldn't take her hand, he engulfed her in a hug.

"It'll be okay," he whispered to her, but she was clearly terrified.

He felt the small trembles that poured through her. Not that he could blame her. If he were in her shoes, he'd have run for the hills by now.

His mother glanced at her watch.

"Jacob? We must go to the restaurant now. I don't want to keep Rosalie waiting."

"Rosalie?" Addy visibly deflated a bit, and Jack saw his mother smirk at the reaction.

"Go get your purse," he told Addy. "Rosalie's excited to see you again. You haven't hung out with her since you two went camping together, right?"

Only he would have noticed Addy's little flush at the mention of camping, but he wasn't about to let his mother make Addy feel inadequate.

"Quite friendly, are they?" his mother asked as Addy went to the bedroom for her purse. "Rosalie and Allison."

"Addison," he said, though he knew she knew her name. "Yeah, they're friends."

"Huh. Odd," his mother said. "Brave of Allison, though. I wouldn't want such a sophisticated, gorgeous woman as Rosalie around my husband."

"Mother, behave," he said, and turned to her with a pointed finger. "Because if you don't, I'm perfectly happy to be motherless."

She balked and her mouth dropped open.

"Ready," Addy said, and held up a little black satin purse she must have also borrowed from Kenzie.

"What a lovely purse, dear," his mum said, without even a hint of sarcasm.

24

I think this is a panic attack.

Addy had never had one before, or at least she didn't think so, but couldn't figure out what else it could be. Ever since she'd spotted Rosalie at the restaurant, already seated and looking like a deer in headlights herself, Addy's heart had started to hammer.

She was simultaneously hot and cold at the same time. Her palms were coated in sweat no matter how many times she wiped them on Kenzie's dress.

Addy could hardly keep track of the conversation. Not that she really needed to. Jack's mom largely ignored both of them to fawn over Rosalie, whom she sat beside.

Jack was pressed against Addy, one hand on her thigh. He squeezed her hand frequently and leaned over to kiss her cheek or whisper compliments in her ear that she quickly forgot.

Any other time, and maybe it would have been comforting. However, it felt more like he was doing it for his mother's sake than hers.

And maybe to make Rosalie jealous, she reminded herself.

Addy took a long swallow of rosé wine and watched Rosalie nod politely at Jack's mom. Whenever she could, Rosalie would steal a look at Addy and give her an *I'm sorry!* look that seemed genuine. But who really knew?

She shrugged and smiled at Rosalie. It probably wasn't her fault that she got roped into this. Still, she had to wonder if Jack was actually the one who'd invited Rosalie, or at least had easily gone along with it.

It was perfect, wasn't it? If his whole goal was to make Rosalie jealous, what better way than to parade his "wife" in front of her along with his mother?

"Sometimes Jacob reminds me so much of his father," Diana said with a sigh. "We sent him to space camp when he was twelve, and you'll never guess…"

Since Diana refused to acknowledge Addy, she didn't bother to listen in on the mundane stories. She felt a twinge of empathy for Rosalie.

It must be terrible to be stuck here listening to stories about your ex while sitting across from his wife, she thought.

The familiar beeping of a hospital pager interrupted Diana's story.

"It's mine," Rosalie said before Jack could reach for his. "I'm so sorry, I have to get back to the hospital."

"Who has the petite filet mignon?" A waiter arrived with four covered plates.

"So soon?" Diana asked. "Can't someone else—"

"Mum, she's a doctor," Jack said. "She's on call. You were a doctor's wife, I know you understand this."

His mother sat back in a huff as Rosalie showered down apologies.

"Don't apologize," Jack told her. "You were kind enough to even show up for this… whatever it is."

Rosalie apologized once again, particularly toward Addy.

"I just… sorry, but I have to go. This was, um, thanks for inviting me," Rosalie said.

She rushed away at a fast clip, and Addy saw Rosalie's slender shoulders loosen and relax with every step away from this mess that she could get. She couldn't blame her. In fact, she was jealous of her.

What I would give to get the hell out of here right now, too.

Diana sighed.

"Poor girl, she can't even enjoy a nice dinner out. Well. At least she has a real career, though," she said.

She eyed her steak without touching it.

"This isn't medium rare," she told the waiter.

"Ma'am, let me cut it open for you and check—"

"I said it's not medium rare. Take it back. So, Addy, tell me again. What do you do?"

I didn't tell you in the first place because you didn't ask.

"I'm, uh, I'm a waitress—"

"She's taken over her father's restaurant," Jack cut in. "Addy is acting as proprietor."

"Hmph. Waitress, restaurant proprietor. Two very different jobs. I can't begin to fathom which is true. Though I have my suspicions," she said and gave Addy a look that chilled her to the marrow.

"Mum, I'm telling you—"

"Jacob, I'm tired. I think I'll have the chauffeur take me to my hotel."

"Your hotel? Mum, you just—"

Diana tossed down two hundred-dollar bills.

"Feel free to take mine to go in a doggy bag," she said pointedly to Addy.

As soon as Diana disappeared from view, Addy couldn't hold it in any longer. She looked to Jack, but when she opened her mouth the only thing that came out was a sob.

"Let's go home," Jack said.

"Where—is everyone leaving?" the waiter asked.

"Yeah, sorry."

"This doesn't cover the bill," the waiter said, accusing. "What are you trying to pull? You can't just order all this and—"

Addy was enveloped in embarrassment and madly wiped at her eyes with her napkin.

"Hail us a cab and run my card," Jack said. "Consider the cash your tip."

"Yes, sir," the waiter said quickly.

"I'm so embarrassed," Addy said as they got into the cab.

"Don't be, my mom is a royal bitch. Always has been. You okay?"

"Just let me be for a minute," she said.

She hated that about herself, how she could barely even speak when she cried. The ride home seemed to take forever with the cab driver unaware of the roadwork being done en route. Jack, thankfully, obliged her and didn't press or ask any questions.

Finally, some peace and quiet, she thought.

However, it gave her time to dwell.

What the hell had he been thinking, springing his bitch of a mom on her? Why did he even have to drag her into it?

One thing was certain. No matter what, if she'd thought they came from totally different worlds before, this confirmed it. She hadn't thought women like his mom actually existed.

Her embarrassment gave way to a fury that was fueled by anxiety.

Who the fuck does he think he is?

When they finally pulled up to the condo, she couldn't get out of the taxi fast enough. Addy slammed the door behind her and left Jack to pay.

Just try to talk to me, she dared him in her head.

She went directly to the bathroom to scrub the makeup off her face and heard the front door shut as she toweled it off.

"Addy?"

She kicked off the too-high heels and barreled into the living room. "What? What do you have to say?"

"What's wrong with you?" he asked, clearly confused. "I warned you, and I told you I was sorry—"

"That doesn't cut it anymore, *Jacob*. I'm not about to be part of your lifestyle choices anymore, okay?"

"Addy, what the hell is the matter with you? What are you talking about?"

"You think your mom's a bitch? You're one to talk. Where do you think you got your whole outlook on life from?"

"What? Don't compare me to my mum—what's gotten into you?"

"I see exactly where this is going." Addy approached him. In her bare feet, she barely reached his shoulder but she was energized by sheer adrenaline. "The second I get to be old hat, you'll just ditch me and move on to the next thing. It's what guys like you do. It's probably what you did to Rosalie, and then—"

"Whoa, hey," he said and pulled himself up to his full height. "I don't know what's gotten into you, but I have zero interest in hearing anything more about Rosalie, and even less about my mum. She's toxic, poisonous, alright? I know that. And I didn't even know she was coming here until an hour before she landed."

"Jack—"

"No, you got to talk, you listen now. Maybe it was shit of me to spring dinner on you like that, but I panicked."

"And Rosalie just magically happened to be there? To get invited? Even if your mom really is the one who invited her, you couldn't—"

"My mum *is* the one who invited her. You can ask Rosalie if you don't believe me. And you're probably right, it wasn't by chance that Rosalie was there. My mum demanded to go directly to the hospital. Hell, for all I know she called ahead to ask if Rosalie was working at the time. She already knew she was here—how she knew, I don't know."

"What? What the hell is wrong with your family? Is your mom stalking you, or what? This is exactly the kind of thing I don't want to be in the middle of. I knew your family had money, but I didn't know... this isn't..."

"Addy." He put his hands on her shoulders. "I don't know what all my mum's been up to. Honestly. But I can tell you one thing. If she knew she'd managed to start a fight between us, that would make her day."

Addy exhaled.

"You're right," she said finally. "I know you're right. But Jack—"

"No more talking."

Addy let out a shriek as he picked her up with ease and tossed her over his shoulder.

"What are you doing—"

"No more talking," he repeated as he carried her to the bedroom.

25

Jack tossed her on the bed and shrugged out of his suit jacket. With her face freshly scrubbed and her hair blown out to reach her waist, she looked young. Innocent. The way she chewed at her lip while she watched him unbuckle his belt didn't hurt, either.

"Come here," he said.

Jack gripped her thighs and pulled her onto her back. He tugged the bottom of the dress up to her abdomen to reveal a slip of a black G-string and matching black thigh highs. Jack reached down and moved the tiny black fabric of her underwear to the side.

She was already wet, but before he could run a thumb across her clit, Addy leaned up on her elbows.

"Are you here to examine me?"

"What?"

"The nurse said a doctor was going to come in and examine me. Are you my doctor?"

Addy looked up at him through her thick lashes with a glint he'd never seen before.

"Uh, yeah," he said.

He didn't think it was possible, but he felt himself grow even harder. The stiffness pushed against the fabric of his trousers.

Addy glanced to the chair in the corner where he'd tossed his coat and stethoscope when he got home. "Where's your coat?"

"What?"

"I thought doctors wore white coats."

He smiled and released her thighs. Jack felt her eyes on him as he slipped into the coat and draped the stethoscope over his neck.

"What brings you in today?" he asked as he turned to face her.

"I'm kind of shy to say."

"It's alright, Miss…"

"Smith," she said quickly.

"Miss Smith. I'm a medical professional, you can tell me."

"Well, doctor, I… I'm a virgin," she said.

"Oh?"

"Yeah, I just turned eighteen… but the thing is, I'm ready to do it. I've been trying to practice. Masturbate, you know? And I just… I'm not sure I'm doing it right."

"I see. And do you know who you're going to 'do it' with?" he asked.

"Not yet," she said with a shake of her head. "I wanted to make sure I could, you know, get myself off first. And then… can I show you?"

"Show me what?"

"How I touch myself. Maybe you can tell me if I'm doing it right."

"Yeah, that… that's a good idea."

Addy reached between her legs and slipped two fingers between her lips. As she pulled the G-string even farther to the side, she slid her fingers across her clit and into the wet folds. She shuddered at her own touch.

Jack stood over her, his cock pressed firm into his trousers. Addy's eyes closed and she moved into an intimate rhythm of her own he'd never seen before. She seemed naked in a way he'd never noticed.

This was her, the real her. He felt honored to be here, to be allowed to watch. She dipped her middle finger into her opening, just enough to add more wetness to her clit.

"That's good," he told her. "How do you taste?"

She brought her fingers to her lips and sucked.

"It's so good," she said. "Sweet. You want to taste?"

"I probably should, just to be certain."

Addy returned her hand to her opening and buried two fingers deep inside.

"Here, doctor," she said, and offered her hand to him. It was warm, as sweet as he remembered.

"Why don't you try playing with your breasts now?"

She grinned up at him and pulled down the black neckline to reveal her hard nipples.

"Like this, doctor?" she asked as she traced her areolas with her fingertips.

"Yeah, just like that," he said. "Miss Smith, I think if we're going to really address your concern, it'll call for a more intensive exam."

"Oh?"

Jack dropped to his knees while Addy slowly circled her clit. "Put your hands over your head."

"Yes, doctor."

As Addy lifted her hands overhead, he pressed her thighs wide apart and licked her sweetness from her opening to her hood in one long stroke. He heard her draw in her breath.

"It's what I suspected," he told her.

"What is it?"

"You're getting yourself off just fine. But you need a good fucking if you really want to feel better." Jack slid a finger into her and Addy instantly pushed against him.

"But doctor, I've never done that before," she said. "I wouldn't even know who to ask."

"No boyfriend?" He started to fuck her faster with his finger while he sucked on her clit.

"No..." she said, breathless. "I'm too busy with cheerleading and homework..."

"Cheerleading and homework," he repeated. "Since you're such a good girl, I can take care of it for you, then. As a medical professional, of course."

"Yes, please, doctor."

Jack rose to his feet and dropped his trousers to the ground. She leaned up and looked at his throbbing length with hunger.

"Can I?" she asked, as she reached for him.

"Have you done this before, Miss Smith?"

"No," she said with a smile. "But I'm a good student. All As."

"I don't doubt it. Can you open your mouth? Stick out your tongue?"

She smiled up at him, flattened her tongue as she stuck it out and said, "Ahh."

"Just stay like that," he said, and slid his tip across the warm wetness of her tongue. "Open…"

"Like this?" She opened her mouth and pulled him to the back of her throat.

"Jesus."

He gasped and raked her hair into a ponytail in his fist. Addy kept her gaze upward as she sucked and licked his cock. Jack wanted to burn this into his memory—the way she looked right then, her cheekbones pronounced and that fire in her eyes.

"That's enough," he said. "I'm—fuck, I'm getting close."

"Did I do good?" she asked as she released him.

"Real good."

Jack reached down, gripped her thighs, and flipped her onto her back. Addy let out a squeal. As he gripped her hips and pulled her toward him, she played with her breasts and held his gaze.

With her legs wrapped around his waist, he teased her with his tip. Addy let out a groan as he slapped her clit with his head, soaked in precum.

"Don't tease me," she said.

"I know what's best for you," he said.

Jack positioned himself at her opening and entered her, just half an inch.

"Yes," Addy gasped. "More."

Jack's thumb pressed into her clit as he entered her slowly, inch by inch. By the time he filled her completely, she panted and squeezed her legs as tightly as she could around him.

"You feel so fucking good," he said.

"Just fuck me."

Jack fell on top of her and began to thrust into her. Addy called out his name, slightly muffled by the white coat. He found her lips and kissed her deep as she clawed at his back. With one hand, she pushed at something close to his shoulder—the stethoscope.

"Don't stop," she urged as he slowed down. "Please don't stop."

"Hold on," he said, and held up the instrument. "Can't diagnose you without checking your heart—"

"Jack, come on, I'm close," she begged.

"Who's Jack? Delirium, even more reason to finish the exam."

"Jack—" she gasped as he pressed the cold metal of the diaphragm to her heart.

He pressed the eartips in and his head filled with her heartbeat. It was already elevated, a fluttering kick.

"Jack, what are you doing?"

He kissed her and she melted against him. Her little gasps and moans made a cacophony along with her heartbeat as he thrust deeper into her.

"You're going to make me come," she whispered.

She didn't have to tell him. Her heart made it clear, a thunder in his head.

"Come for me," he said.

"Is that... fuck, is that an order?" Her heartbeat jumped up again. "A doctor's order?"

"Come for me, Addy."

He'd never heard such a hammering before. As Addy's wails filled the room, as he felt the clenching of her center and the rush of wetness from between her legs, her heart battered wildly, filled his head entirety with her.

"Jack," she called, and clutched him closer.

I fucking love you, he thought as her heart began to slow. *I love you, Addy.*

But somehow, the words wouldn't come out.

26

Addy sighed as she pulled into the restaurant. She checked her text messages from Jack, who had spent his morning seeing his mother off at the airport. At the moment, he was texting Addy a hilarious play by play of the whole deal as he started his shift at the hospital.

Addy pursed her lips, and figured that she ought to check in with Kenzie.

How's Dad doing? Addy texted Kenzie.

Even though Addy was the one doing the scheduling, it seemed like she and Kenzie crossed paths briefly during the day. Addy was pulling the morning shifts and Kenzie preferred the evenings, perfecting her flirtations to rake in hefty tips.

OK, I think, Kenzie replied. *Sleeps a lot.*

How's the drinking?

About the same. I tried to water down the bottles, but he can tell so just drinks more and yells at me.

Addy sighed again but plastered on a smile as she got out of her car and entered the restaurant.

"Addy! Thank God you're here." Dawn zoomed toward her, her eyes wild. "Both the dishwashers called in sick today. Both of them! And you know it's just because of the homecoming game—"

"What about the guys for the dinner shift?" Addy quickly calculated how busy the morning would be.

They could get by if they switched the dishwashing machine to quick cycles, but just barely.

"Same. The same guys were scheduled for doubles."

"I'll call Kenzie." Addy pulled out her phone and braced for Kenzie's complaints.

"What? You want me to play *dishwasher*? I don't think so. That's gross and there are no tips."

"Kenzie, I'm not going to beg you and this isn't a favor. This is Mom and Dad's restaurant. Get your ass in here within an hour."

Kenzie hung up on her, but Addy knew she'd be there. And Addy already knew she'd be splitting her tips with her baby sister to appease her.

"Chef says there's no avocados." One of the new girls approached Addy with her head cocked sideways.

"Of course there are avocados, I saw them arrive yesterday."

"I mean no *good* avocados."

"They're all bad?"

The girl shrugged. Addy rushed to the back even as she heard Dawn unlock the front door and the rustle of the first customers arrive.

"Ethan! What's wrong with the avocados?" she yelled as she flew past the cook to the fridge.

"All rotten on the inside or with pits so big the meat's useless," he called back. "What am I subbing?"

"I'll let you know. Probably spinach."

"Regulars ain't gonna like that."

"I know, but a vegetable isn't going to kill them. Can you prep some creamed spinach? Make it unhealthy enough and they won't grumble so much."

"You got it, boss."

She reapplied the smile to her face and wrapped the black apron strings around her waist twice. A Friday morning breakfast rush was mild compared to the weekends, but the stodgy group of elderly regulars would keep her on her toes.

Addy was on autopilot as she flew around the restaurant, refilling coffee mugs and explaining the avocado situation to huffy guests. One woman, a local but not a regular, rolled her eyes aghast when she heard about the avocado crisis. Her neatly trimmed silver bob reminded Addy of Diana.

Thank God I never have to see that beastly woman again, she thought.

But the specter of her so-called mother-in-law managed to put a damper on her for days after the event. She'd be taking an order and suddenly the image of the Aussie prima donna would appear in her mind's eye.

I have to admit, with a mother like that it's amazing Jack turned out as relatively normal as he did.

If she had any doubts that this whole fake marriage was a bad idea, Diana sealed it. Still, every time Jack texted her she felt a flutter in her heart.

During her ten-minute break when she locked herself in her car to zone out to music and not get pulled into restaurant drama, he sent her a picture of him and Philip at work digging into a homebaked pie one of the nurses had brought. Addy's face lit up. It was just what she needed to face the last half of her shift.

"You owe me. Big time," Kenzie said as Addy slipped through the kitchen. Kenzie had yellow gloves up to her elbows and a face mask covered half her face. "Kenzie, it's dirty dishes, not a biohazard."

"Same thing. You've seen some of those people eat. So gross. You know I found dentures on one of the plates? Dentures, Addy!"

"Did you... did you keep them?"

"Hell, no! I threw them away and then had to change gloves. By the way, you need to order more of these."

"You threw them away? Kenzie, those things cost thousands of dollars."

"Then they shouldn't leave them on dirty plates," Kenzie said with a shrug.

"Kenzie, what was Dad doing when you left?"

"I dunno. Sleeping, I think. He was on the chair."

Addy looked at her watch. Her shift was up and her feet throbbed. All she wanted to do was go home and climb into bed, but with Kenzie working the evening shift she didn't want to leave her dad alone for that long of a stretch.

"I have a temporary dishwasher coming in to change you out," she said. "He's on loan from Dusty's. Text me when he gets here? I'm going to swing by the house and check on Dad."

"Yeah, yeah," Kenzie muttered as she scrubbed uselessly at omelet remains.

When Addy pulled up to her dad's house, she saw that Kenzie had forgotten to close the garage door.

"Goddamnit, Kenzie," she said aloud. The last thing they needed was for someone to burglarize the place.

She heard her father's monstrous snores as soon as she walked in. The house was still somewhat clean from when her dad had been in the hospital, but it was clearly heading back to disaster territory.

"Dad?" she called, but his snores remained steady.

He was passed out in his chair with what looked like a watered-down whiskey in a tumbler on the table. Addy put a crocheted blanket over him, picked up the glass and wiped away the water mark.

She could tell by his slack jaw he was down deep. It would be pointless to try and wake him.

In the kitchen, she opened the dishwasher after she rinsed the glass, but it overflowed with dirty dishes. None of them had been rinsed.

"Screw it," she said. "Kenzie and him can deal with this."

Any other day, she would have rinsed what was in the dishwasher and started the load.

Let them fend for themselves for once, she thought as she put the tumbler in the sink.

She tried to put Diana, Kenzie, and her dad out of her mind as she drove home.

Home, she thought. *That still seems weird.*

Addy smiled when she saw Jack's Jeep in his spot.

"Jack?" she called as she entered, but the condo was dark and silent. "Jack?"

She opened the bedroom door to find him already in bed asleep.

Addy kicked off her black clogs and stripped down to the boy shorts she wore under her work skirt and the tight tank top underneath the button-up. He roused as she snuggled up against him.

"Hey," he said, his voice thick with sleep.

Addy pushed her back against him and made herself the little spoon in their pair. As Jack rolled toward her, he wrapped one thick arm around her waist. She felt his hardness against her ass and her body responded as his hand roamed up her stomach to her breasts.

"It wasn't right how you treated Rosalie."

Jack stopped. "What?"

"The way you treated her... all of it. I'm afraid that, you know, one day you'll do the same thing to me."

It was easier like this, telling him her deepest fears while she faced away from him.

"Addy, she left me because I didn't propose to her. It's not really an issue here. I mean, we're kind of way past that."

"I'm telling you that I'm afraid of something," she said. Addy could feel the heat of his breath on her neck. "It's your job to comfort me."

Jack hooked a thumb in the waist of her tight little shorts and inched them down. "Jack—"

"Shh."

She let him roll up her tank top to the top of her breasts, the pressure from the tight material making them swell and pucker below the hem. Jack opened her legs easily and tested her wetness with his finger.

"You're always so fucking wet," he whispered into her ear.

Before she could respond, he'd disappeared under the covers and she felt his tongue trace across her mound while his hands explored her breasts. As his mouth reached her clit, she gasped and her eyes shot open.

Addy wove her fingers through his hair and held him against her. She could see nothing but the moving sheet between her legs, but when she felt his finger against her opening she pushed instinctively against him.

As she panted toward orgasm, there was a dim thought in the back of her mind. It wasn't exactly what she'd had in mind when she'd asked for comfort, but she had to admit it felt pretty fucking good.

She opened her legs wider, unable to get enough of him. Suddenly, he stopped. Addy squirmed against the discomfort, gripped his head tighter and presented herself to him. "Say my name," he demanded from between her thighs.

"Jack," she said, and his tongue flicked across her clit.

The more she said his name, the louder, the more pleasure he gave her. When she finally came against his tongue, her heart pounded inside her head so loudly she could have sworn it shook the room.

It wasn't until she was coming down from the high that she realized it was the neighbor. A faint pounding sounded from the living room wall along with murmured exasperated sounds.

"Looks like you pissed off the neighbors," Jack said as he emerged from the sheets, her wetness spread across his face.

"Who cares?" she asked as he spooned her again. "They're probably just jealous. Who knows the last time they got laid?"

"For all we know, it might be Jeremy."

Addy hadn't considered that. Surprisingly, she also didn't care.

27

"Jack?"

Nurse Bostian popped his head into the hospital's break room. "There's a Mr. Fuller here to see you? I'm sorry, the front desk tried to have him see someone else, but he was really... adamant."

"Ted Fuller?" Jack asked, his mouth still half-full with a stale sandwich from the cafeteria.

"Uh, yeah."

"I'll be right there."

"He's in room 2-E."

Jack dumped the rest of his lunch in the trash and rushed down the hall. When he opened the door, Addy's dad looked the same as he remembered.

Years of alcohol abuse gave people a certain type of pallid expression, a hunched-over look, that made them look years older than they were.

"Mr. Fuller, what brings you in?" he asked.

"It's my heart."

"How so?"

"It feels... kind of the same thing as last time," he said.

As Jack approached him, he was nearly knocked over by the smell of whiskey. He couldn't tell if it had spilled on him, was just his breath, or a little of both.

"Can you describe the sensation? Sharp, dull? Where exactly is it?"

Addy's dad pointed to the center of his chest.

"It kind of comes and goes in waves," he said. "Sometimes it's sharp when it's, you know, at the peak, and then it subsides to a more dull throbbing kind of pain."

Jack removed his stethoscope from his neck and gestured for Mr. Fuller to unbutton his shirt.

"This'll be cold," he said. "Can you take your shirt off completely? I need to listen from your back. Sit up straight."

When the shirt was removed, the stench of body odor mixed with whiskey was almost unbearable. Jack listened to the heartbeat, a bit fast, but regular and nowhere in the realm of unusual.

"Sounds solid," he said. "As I recall, from your last hospital stay there was nothing found in your bloodwork. I'll take another look at those records though. For now, I think we should order a full blood workup just to rule anything out."

"What... what do you think it is? A heart attack?"

"I can't say for sure, but I don't think so," Jack said.

"Are you... are you gonna tell Addison?"

"Addison?" Jack asked as he made order notes. "Not unless you want me to."

"No," he said quickly. "Let's just leave her and Kenzie out of it."

"Whatever you say. A nurse is going to come in and take care of the blood orders soon. Once they get back, I'll go over them and discuss the results with you and we'll go from there. Sound good?"

"How long will that be?"

"Hard to say, the nurse will have a better time estimate than me. However, things seem to go a little faster in the ER, and it hasn't been too busy today."

"Okay," he said slowly as he shrugged on the flannel shirt.

It took three hours for the blood results to come back.

"Well?" Jack asked the nurse as he handed over the results.

"Nothing too out of line," the nurse said with a shrug. "He's a drunk, right? I mean—"

"Thanks," Jack said quickly.

He scanned the results. Surprisingly, for a man who drank his calories and otherwise subsisted on red meat whenever he could, he was relatively healthy. However, the B-type natriuretic peptide protein was slightly elevated.

Jack had expected it to be higher given the years of alcohol abuse, but it was still technically within a "worry-free" range.

"That took a long while," Mr. Fuller said when Jack knocked on the door.

"Actually, that was speedy in ER time," Jack said.

"Okay, give it to me," he said. "What's wrong?"

"Your bloodwork is largely normal," Jack said. "There's a small elevation of the B-type natriuretic pep—"

"English, doc."

"It's a protein that's produced by the heart. It's high, but not at a dangerous level. At this point, it's something to keep an eye on. Maybe go see your GP and retest it in a month. I, uh, would recommend laying off any drinking until then because alcohol can exacerbate it."

"You, uh, you doctors aren't allowed to tell people that I was here, right? That's what you meant when I asked about Addison?"

"Well, no... doctor-patient confidentiality," Jack said reluctantly.

He clutched the results tighter in his hands. The bloodwork might be in the normal range, but he still had a bad feeling about it.

That's just what the medical field needs, he thought. *Intuition.*

"Let's just keep our lips zipped then," Mr. Fuller said. He stood up and wobbled slightly. "This is something for us menfolk to worry about. Besides, I'm sure it's nothing. That's what the tests say, right? Nothing?"

"Basically," Jack said slowly.

"Well, thanks, I guess," Mr. Fuller said. "Think maybe I'm just still a little spooked after that last incident."

"Better safe than sorry," Jack said. "It's always wise to come in if you suspect something's up."

As he watched Mr. Fuller head down the hall toward the exit, he paused only briefly before he ran after him. "Mr. Fuller? How did you get here?"

"Taxi," he said gruffly.

"My shift is just about over. Would you like a ride home?"

"That sounds real nice, doc. Thank you."

"Okay, just… just wait right here. I'll be back in ten minutes."

The ride to Addison's house—her old house—was largely quiet. Mr. Fuller was a man of few words.

I can't believe he doesn't know we're married. Where does he think Addy's living?

"You single, doc?" he asked suddenly as they pulled up to the house.

"Uh… well…"

"Hell, you're young. 'Course you are. Have fun with it. But just so you know? When it comes time to settle down, you're not gonna find nobody better than my Addison."

"I don't doubt that, sir," Jack said. He couldn't help the smile that tugged at his face.

"If and when the time comes, you just let me know. She can be feisty and stubborn, but underneath it all she's got a heart of gold. Takes after her mother in that way."

"Take care of yourself, Mr. Fuller," Jack said.

As he watched Addy's dad climb the steps, he briefly wondered if he should escort him in.

And then what? Become his volunteer caretaker?

He shook his head and pulled away. When he walked in the door, Addy was curled up on the couch streaming *Stranger Things*.

"Come here," she said. "I just started the second season."

She opened up the blanket she was buried under and he slipped out of his shoes to join her.

Any thought of telling her about her dad disappeared when she reached beneath his scrubs.

"I thought you wanted to watch the show," he said from behind her.

"And I thought you knew what Netflix and chill meant," she said. "You smell like hospital."

"Is that a good thing?"

"I dunno. To me it just smells like you now."

She gripped him in her fist while he lifted up her skirt to find nothing but soft, bare skin underneath.

"Were you planning this?" he asked and kissed her neck from behind.

"Maybe." He reached for her to turn her toward him, but she resisted. "No. From behind."

Addy guided his tip toward her and he gritted his teeth at the heat of her entrance. She lifted her top leg and wrapped it across his calf to pull him toward her. With one hand she clung to the couch cushion. The other was between her legs where she played with her clit.

Jack went along with it, although as he entered her he couldn't help but remember the way Mr. Fuller had touched his chest.

It's my heart. Addy began to pant and push her ass against him.

He grabbed her hip and thrust into her. Something wasn't right, but he couldn't figure it out.

The tests were mostly normal. He'd seen much worse results in other patients that still didn't call for delving deeper.

"Fuck me harder," Addy moaned and pulled him back into the moment.

He leaned toward her and bit her shoulder as he changed angles to glide against her G-spot.

Maybe it really was nothing, he told himself.

Alcoholics and drug addicts, some of them were nearly indestructible. It was like they'd built up such a tolerance they nearly had superhero powers, coming back from the literal dead with surprising regularity.

"Make me come," Addy groaned.

He reached for her nipple and rolled it between his fingers.

She responded with calls of his name. Normally that would put him over the edge, make him feel like she belonged to him, but what had happened with her dad made him nearly a spectator.

"Come on," Addy said. "Make me come."

Jack slid his hand down her toned stomach and brushed her hand away. He pushed against her clit and made her cry out.

"Yeah," she said. "Like that. Faster."

Jack obliged, followed her directions, and fucked her the way he knew she liked it. The way he knew would make her orgasm hard and fast.

As he felt her come, the walls of her insides clenching and releasing his hard length, he watched Winona Ryder's face over Addy's shoulder. She looked scared and confused.

"You didn't come," Addy said, sleepy and disappointed over her shoulder.

"Oh, uh, sorry. It was a long day."

"What can I do?" she asked. "Come on, I want you to feel good."

Addy started to lower herself on the couch. As he felt her tongue on his tip, her lips wrapped around his cock, he closed his eyes and willed the picture of her dad from his mind.

It took twenty minutes, but when he finally released himself into the back of her throat, he'd completely forgotten about the old man's heart.

28

"What's Jack doing on his day off?" Dawn asked.

Addy dumped the tray of dirty dishes in the sink and wiped her brow.

"Shopping for some kind of jet ski thing," she said. "And you know what that means. The next time we both have a day off, he's going to drag me off on that death trap."

"You don't know how lucky you are," Dawn said. "I'm lucky to get a night out that's more exciting than a movie and dinner at Dusty's."

Addy laughed. "Maybe you're right."

"Addy?" The girl who'd just come on for the lunch shift stuck her head in back. "There's a call for you. It's… it's the hospital?"

"The hospital? But Jack's not there …" Addy headed to the cash register and picked up the landline, confused. "Jack? What are you doing at work?"

"Addison Fuller?" the woman asked. She didn't recognize the voice.

"Yes, that's me. Is Jack okay? What's—"

"Is Theodore Fuller your father?"

"Yes." Her blood turned to ice. *Of course it was Dad. Of course.* "What happened?"

"He came to the ER in an ambulance and has been moved to the ICU."

"Is he okay? He's in the ICU, so that means he's okay, right?" Addy whipped off her apron even as she spoke.

"Your father has cardiomyopathy."

"What... what is that? Like a heart attack?"

"It's when the heart becomes enlarged, and... are you able to come in right now? I can't tell you much over the phone, it's best you talk to a doctor."

"Yeah, yes, I'm coming," she said and slammed down the phone.

"Everything okay?" Dawn asked. Addy jumped at the voice.

"No, my dad—he's in the hospital. Can you cover for me?"

"Sure, yeah," Dawn said. "Go, we've got this."

Addy pulled out her phone as she ran toward the car. Briefly, she paused, not knowing who to call first.

Jack or Kenzie? But when she opened her call app, it was Jack's name she tapped.

"Hey!" he said. "I'm glad you called. I can't decide between the Ski-Doo—"

"Where are you? Are you in town?"

"Yeah, some place on Pine. Are you okay? What happened?"

"My dad's in the ICU."

"I'm on my way. Are you driving there? Do I need to pick you up?"

"I'm driving, I'm leaving the restaurant now."

"Did they say what it was?"

"Cardio—something. I can't remember."

"I'll meet you there."

Addy flipped the phone to speaker mode and dialed Kenzie.

"Addy, you better have a really good reason for waking me up," Kenzie said, groggy. "I have the whole day off and I'm not—"

"Dad's in the hospital."

"What?" The sleep disappeared from Kenzie's voice.

"Where were you?"

"Where was I?"

"Kenzie, goddamnit! He took an ambulance to the ER, where were you?"

"I... hold on," she said with a whisper. "I'm at a friend's place.

Hey," Kenzie whispered to someone. "What's the address of this place?"

Addy could hear a deep male voice reply.

"Kenzie! How long will it take you to get to the hospital?"

"I, um. I think my car's here. What! We're in Indian Hills? Addy, it'll take... a little while. I'm leaving now."

Addy hung up before she could say anything more. Or burst into tears. Whatever came first.

How many nights was Kenzie hooking up with random guys and leaving Dad alone?

She never should have moved out. That was obvious. Now look at what had happened. And she couldn't even blame Kenzie, since her sister had never had a speck of responsibility.

It was on her. Whatever happened to her dad, it was all her fault.

Jack was already there when she pulled up to the hospital. He paced in front of the doors.

"Jack! Did you see him? Check on him? Is he—"

"I did, briefly. He's asleep right now, but stable."

"Can I see him?"

"They're not letting anybody see him right now."

"But you're a doctor here! Can't you—"

"I don't make the rules, though," he said. "Come with me, we'll talk to the doctor who's been handling the case since he was transferred to ICU."

He grabbed her hand and led her into the brightly lit hospital.

"But can't you be his doctor? Can't you—"

"One thing at a time, Addy," he said. He sounded so confident, so sure, that it made her fall quiet.

"Addison Fuller?" the doctor asked.

She'd never seen him before, but his age and stature were soothing. He must have been in his fifties and his white coat fell almost to his knees. Thanks to Jack, she knew that the longer the white coat, the more experienced the doctor.

"Yeah, that's me," she said. She didn't even bother to correct the surname.

"Your father had cardiomyopathy. It's when the heart gets bigger and thicker, and in turn weaker. It's often worsened by excessive alcohol use, although age and genetics are usually the primary cause. Your father's blood alcohol level was almost three times the legal limit when he was admitted. It's... quite shocking, really, that he was even conscious let alone had the wherewithal to call an ambulance."

"Jesus," Addy said.

She faltered, and Jack caught her elbow to lower her into one of the chairs in the waiting room. Vaguely, Addy was aware of all the people around her. Some stared at her, while others were wrapped up in their own pains and traumas.

"Miss Fuller? Are you alright?" the doctor asked.

"Yeah, sorry."

"Does your father have a history of alcohol abuse?"

"Yes," she said meekly, embarrassed.

"We also tested his liver, given the BAC levels and cardiomyopathy, and it looks like your father is in the middle stages of alcoholic liver disease. Not all alcoholics develop this," he continued.

Addy flushed at the word "alcoholic." It sounded like it rang out through the waiting room.

"However, it's more common in those who also have poor nutrition. Miss Fuller, I have to tell you, your father is on the border of developing liver cirrhosis."

"What... what does that mean?" She was aware of Jack's hand wrapped around hers, but the comfort it offered was minimal.

"Well, up until cirrhosis, the liver is able to repair itself. In early stages the symptoms are barely noticeable, if at all. Unfortunately, this means that the liver can become damaged beyond repair before the patient is aware of the problem."

"But you said he's borderline. So it can be fixed, right? His liver can still fix itself?"

"Anything is possible," the doctor said. "But in my opinion, I don't think that's likely. I believe this event might have pushed him over the edge and when we retest I foresee him to be in full cirrhosis."

"No," Addy said as she shook her head. "No."

"Also, we tested his gamma-glutamyl transpeptidase, or GGT, which is an enzyme linked to the liver. His levels are extremely high, which is another sign of toxic alcohol levels as well as cholestatic damage."

"I don't know what all that means," Addy said.

"It furthers my diagnosis that I believe your father is moving swiftly into late stage liver damage coupled with cardiomyopathy that can lead to a heart attack at any moment."

"How... how could I not know?" she asked. "He seemed fine, just the other day..."

"It's not your fault," Jack said.

The doctor flipped through his notes. "It says here in his charts that Mr. Fuller was here two days ago complaining of chest pains. And that you saw him, Dr. Stratton."

The doctor looked at Jack curiously.

"What?" Addy dropped his hand and turned to Jack. "Is this true?"

"Addy, I—"

"Why didn't you tell me?"

"Your father asked me not to, and I—I couldn't, Addy. Legally."

"So, what, you just sent him on his merry way? He's *dying*, Jack! And he was here asking for your help, what, two days ago? This is your fault!" she screamed, and in the darkest corner of her heart she believed it.

"Addy, his blood work came back fine—"

"Yeah, well, apparently you weren't supposed to be testing his fucking blood, Jack! It was his liver. *This* doctor figured it out."

"Addy! Jack! Oh my God, is everything okay? Where is he?" Kenzie came barreling down the hall in a barely-there minidress, barefoot with heels in her hands and last night's makeup streaked across her face.

"No, it's not!" Addy yelled.

"What—"

"You deal with this," she said, and shoved the printouts the doctor had given her into Kenzie's hands. "Both of you, you fucking deal with this for once."

"Addy—" Jack started, but she was already half-running down the hall.

"What happened?" she could hear Kenzie call.

"Addy!" Jack caught up to her outside. She wasn't aware there were tears that poured down her face until he grabbed her elbow and spun her around. "Calm down! I know you're upset, but—"

"Calm down? Don't tell me to calm down! That's my *dad*, Jack! And I left him, I... I fucking moved out and stopped taking care of him so I could play house with you. How ridiculous is that?"

"This isn't my fault—"

"Then whose fault is it, Jack?"

He opened his mouth, but she held up her hand.

"Don't you dare say it's mine."

Jack took a deep breath. "Addy, you stay here."

"What?"

"You stay. Go talk to Kenzie. I'll leave."

"Where are you go—"

"Stay with your family. I'll leave," he repeated.

Before she could ask anything else, he turned on his heels and walked into the parking lot.

"Addy! What happened?" Kenzie was at her side and pulled at her arm. "Is Dad okay? Did I do this?"

Addy sucked in her breath.

"It's not your fault," she told Kenzie halfheartedly. She wrapped an arm around her sister and escorted her back inside.

A voice deep inside her already mourned what she'd done to Jack.

Fuck, she thought, *there's no way he's coming back now.*

29

"I'm sorry," Kenzie sniffed.

"Stop saying that," Addy said.

"But I am!"

"Kenzie, we've been here for five hours and you must have said it five hundred times. Dad was an alcoholic, okay? Is. He would have destroyed his liver whether you went out last night or not."

"But I could have been there," Kenzie whined. "I could have cut him off, maybe—"

"When's the last time Dad let anyone get between him and his whiskey?" Addy asked.

As she tried to calm Kenzie down, she had to admit it worked for her, too. Being forced to be reasonable for Kenzie's sake made her see things from a different perspective.

It's not our job to be his caretaker, to tell him when and what he can drink.

"Addison and Kenzie Fuller?" A nurse they hadn't spoken to before approached them. Her shoes clicked against the linoleum.

"Yes?" Addy asked as Kenzie jumped up.

"The doctor has approved family visitors, but only for a few minutes. Your dad's awake, but very groggy." The nurse touched Addy's forearm. "Just a warning. He doesn't look very good and he might be... confused."

Kenzie shot her a look. *Confused and doesn't look good. We're used to that.*

But the nurse's warning didn't prepare her for what she saw. Their dad had so many wires that popped out of him he looked part machine. His watery blue eyes shot toward them as they entered, but he didn't move his head.

"Addison? MacKenzie?" he asked, as if he weren't certain.

"It's us, Dad," Kenzie said and rushed toward him.

Another nurse that had been checking his vitals glanced at them.

"You're his daughters?" she asked. Addy nodded. "I'll give you a couple of minutes, but I need to come back soon to finish up."

"My heart…" he said, but Addy shook her head.

"It doesn't matter."

His eyes glazed over and although he looked in her direction, it was like he looked straight through her. "Thirsty…"

"Here, Dad," Kenzie said, and held up a paper cup of water by his bed. "There's water right here."

He shook his head slightly, but it looked pained. "Drink…"

"Yeah, Dad, there's water right here," Kenzie said. "Do you want me to hold it up for you?"

"Bottle…"

"He wants whiskey, Kenzie," Addy snapped.

Her dad nodded vigorously.

"Oh. No, Dad, sorry. You're in the hospital. You can't have that here. Try the water…"

He gathered up a reserve of strength and knocked it out of her sister's hand. "Dad, stop!" Addy said.

"Janice?" For a moment his eyes cleared and locked on Addy's.

"Dad—" she started.

"Janice, so beautiful."

"He thinks you're Mom," Kenzie whispered loudly.

"Yeah, I get that, Kenzie. Dad, Mom is—"

"Where the girls, Jan?"

"Dad—"

"Addy and Kenzie, they okay?"

Addy felt tears well at the corners of her eyes, but she blinked them back. "They're good," she said. "Addy and Kenzie are fine."

"Where… Jan, where are they? Want to see them…"

"They're on the way. They're coming right now."

"Okay. That's good," he said. "Janice, you look real pretty."

"Thanks," Addy said. She looked to Kenzie, but her sister was frozen. Silent tears rolled down her cheeks.

"Tired," he said.

"You should rest. Get some sleep."

"Okay. Love you."

"I love you, too," Addy said as she forced the waver out of her voice.

"I love you, Dad," Kenzie said.

As her sister touched his shoulder, the machines started to blare. The nurse rushed into the room with another nurse in pink scrubs on her heels.

"BP is dropping," she said as she lifted his arm and punched a pattern into the machine. The nurse barked to the pink-suited nurse, "Get a doctor."

"What's happening?" Kenzie cried. "Is he okay? What's—"

"I need you both to wait outside," the nurse said. She barely looked up.

"No! We're not—"

"Outside *now*." Addy grabbed her sister's arm and dragged her into the hallway.

"Addy, stop! Dad needs us! He's—"

"Dad's gone, Kenzie," Addy said.

She listened to Kenzie blubber and sob. "How do you know? They didn't say that. You can't give up on him…"

Addy guided Kenzie toward the corner of the waiting room and wrapped her arm around her. Kenzie cried into her shoulder, soaked her shirt. For some reason it reminded her of when they were kids and one of the neighbors had cut off Kenzie's favorite Barbie's hair into a mohawk.

As tears tracked down her face, she thought of how she'd been strong for Kenzie then. Damn if she wouldn't do the same now.

"Addison? MacKenzie?" The same older doctor that had met her with Jack loomed over them. "I'm sorry, but your father's heart stopped. We tried everything to revive him, but it was just too weakened by the cardiomyopathy."

Kenzie began to keen, and Addy massaged her shoulder gently.

"Thank you for trying," Addy said, holding in a sob.

"If it's any consolation, he went quick and painlessly. If it weren't for the heart condition... cirrhosis is often a very long, drawn-out and painful disease. It... I hope this doesn't sound crude, but it could be seen as a blessing."

"A blessing?" Kenzie said as she looked up from Addy's shirt. "Are you fucking kidding me?"

The doctor stiffened and looked away. "Someone will be by soon to talk about next steps with you."

"Thanks," Addy said quietly.

"Next steps? What does he mean next steps?" Kenzie asked.

"I mean... I guess... what to do with the body? I don't know, I've never done this before."

"What... what *do* we do with it?" Kenzie asked.

"I don't know," Addy repeated.

Two hours passed, and both girls cried most of their tears out. Addy felt hollow and empty, like a dishrag that had been wrung out.

Finally, with Kenzie's nagging, Addy approached the receptionist.

"Excuse me? My father just... just died. And we were told to wait—"

"Yes, Mrs. Stratton," the receptionist said. "The hospital mortician is on his way right now to get you."

"Oh. Thanks." Addy examined the woman's face, but she didn't recognize her. But clearly, the woman knew her as Jack's wife.

When she returned to Kenzie, there was a thin, pale, balding man standing over her. The epitome of a mortician.

"Addison Fuller?" he asked and turned to her.

"Yes." She was taken aback by his sharp features.

"I'm Craig Sanders, the hospital mortician on duty. The remains have been transported to the on-site mortuary. I'll need one or both of you to formally identify the body."

"Identify... yeah, it's our dad," Kenzie said. "We were literally in there talking to him when he... when he..."

"I understand this seems strange and outdated, but it's required," Mr. Sanders said.

"Oh, um, okay?"

"Follow me." He walked at a surprisingly fast pace that made both of them half jog after him.

It had only been a few hours, but their father's body looked almost cartoonishly lifeless. Addy had always thought the dead would look like they were sleeping, but that wasn't the case.

It was almost magical how obvious it was that there was no life left. Kenzie let out a small cry, but no tears fell. She was all cried out.

"Is this your father's body, Theodore Fuller?" Mr. Sanders asked.

"Yes," Addy said.

"Sign here."

She scribbled her name where he pointed, unaware of what the paper said. Kenzie reached out to their father's arm as she handed the pen back.

"Don't touch him, Kenzie," she said quickly.

"Why not?"

"Your sister's probably right," Mr. Sanders said. "It can be disorienting. Cold and stiff. But you're welcome to, if you'd like."

Kenzie shivered. "Never mind."

"This way," Mr. Sanders said, and escorted them into what looked like any other office. It could have been a CPA's or attorney's.

"So, what's next?" Addy said. She was comforted by kicking into planning mode.

"Are you working with a funeral director?" Mr. Sanders asked.

Kenzie let out a strange laugh.

"No," Addy said. "We weren't... exactly planning this—"

"I understand. Is there a specific church or other faith-based institute you'd like to handle the final proceedings?"

"No," Addy said. "Dad isn't—wasn't—religious."

"That's fine. Do you know if your father had a will? Or other legal document that stipulated his wishes?"

"I... I don't know," Addy said. "I don't think so. But, he'd want to be buried next to Mom."

"Yeah," Kenzie said. She nodded quickly. "Next to Mom."

"Alright, and do you know the name of the cemetery or mausoleum?"

"It's just the one on the hill," Addy said. "You know? The big one."

"And what was your mother's name?"

"Janice Fuller."

"Alright." Mr. Sanders made a note. "Addison, are you the administrator of your father's estate?"

"I... I guess so?"

"Will the body be cremated prior to burial?"

"Is that something I have to decide now?"

"Not right away. But the doctor on staff does need to know. It's required information on the medical certificate so you can register the death. Registration is required within five days."

Addy looked toward Kenzie.

"Yeah," her sister said. "Cremation. He... I don't want him to be buried where all the bugs and... just cremate him. Okay?"

"Okay," Addy said. "Cremation."

"Alright," Mr. Sanders said and made another note. "Do you know if your father would have wanted his organs donated prior to cremation?"

"I, uh, I don't think he felt strongly about that," Addy said.

"I don't know if anyone would want them," Kenzie said quietly.

"Kenzie!"

"That's a common mistake," Mr. Sanders said quickly. "Quite a bit of remains can be utilized for donation. Tissue, corneas—"

"We get it," Addy said. "Well, I guess? I mean, yes, you have my permission if there's anything... you know, that can be used..."

"Alright, then," Mr. Sanders said. "If you'd like, the hospital works with an excellent funeral director who can serve as the liaison. He can set up arrangements with the cemetery, discuss memorial options with you if that would be of interest, and recommend bereavement counseling."

"Thanks," Addy said.

"Right this way, and we'll get you the medical certificate and connect you with the funeral director."

30

Addy's hands shook as she zipped up the black dress. It had been her mother's, and she'd forgotten about it entirely.

Only after she'd dismissed everything in her closet as not formal enough—and everything in Kenzie's closet as too suggestive—did she venture into her parents' old bedroom. Shoved in the far back was the knee-length black cocktail dress with sleeves to the elbow and a square neckline trimmed in pearls.

When she'd found it, she brought the dress to her face and inhaled. Part of her thought that, somehow, it would still smell like her mom. But it smelled of nothing at all.

"Addy, can you zip me up?" Kenzie wandered into the room in a slinky black dress that barely covered her ass.

Black fishnet stockings hugged her legs.

"Is that what you—sure," Addy corrected herself. Kenzie held up her auburn hair as Addy squeezed her sister into the dress.

"Thanks," Kenzie said, and disappeared down the hall.

"We leave in twenty!" Addy called after her.

She looked in the mirror and gasped. Her mother stared back at her. Even with the dark circles under her eyes from the past five days of fitful sleep, she couldn't deny it.

Actually, it made her look even more like her mother. So

many of her memories involved her mother being sick, and those dark half moons below her eyes were eerily familiar.

Addy had been shocked at how quickly the hospital and the funeral director had pulled everything together. It was also so matter-of-fact and professional. Of course, that made sense. It was a business, and her father's death was one of scores they probably handled every week.

With Kenzie by her side, they'd been herded through countless questions and options. Addy had steeled herself in preparation for avoiding the common pitfalls she'd heard about.

Funeral directors that tried to guilt grieving daughters into upgrading to a ten-thousand-dollar cherry wood coffin because "their loved one deserved it." Addy knew she wouldn't fall for the trap, but she had no idea how Kenzie would react.

Fortunately, the funeral director at the hospital was far from a salesperson. She simply stated the starting options and was always upfront about prices. The only issue Kenzie struggled with was the coffin.

"He's cremated, Kenz," Addy had said.

"So?" Kenzie had looked to the funeral director for confirmation. "Cremated people can still have coffins, can't they?"

"You can certainly do whatever you like. Coffin or no coffin, but both are possible."

"Kenzie, what's the point in a coffin?"

"Mom had a coffin," Kenzie pointed out.

"How did you—I didn't think you remembered that."

"You didn't think I remembered Mom's funeral?"

"We'll take a coffin," Addy had said.

"May I recommend the basic model?" the funeral director asked, keenly aware of Addy's trepidation about the process. "It will serve the purpose just fine for the memorial service, and of course if you'd like to work with a florist they can accommodate as well."

"Sure," Addy said. "Let's do that."

"As for the remains, an option with cremation is to bury part of the remains and keep part. Is that something you're interested in?"

She could see Kenzie looking at her from the corner of her eye.

"No... not for me at least," Addy said. "Kenzie?"

Kenzie bit her lip and slowly shook her head. "No, he'd want to be by Mom. And it feels weird to me, separating it like that—"

"Okay," the funeral director said.

Addy shook her head at the swiftness of the process. She opened the closet in her old bedroom to find shoes, but realized all she had were beat-up sneakers.

Shit. All my decent clothes and shoes are at Jack's.

But she'd be damned if she was going to call him up on the day of her father's funeral and ask if she could come by for shoes.

"Hey, Kenzie!"

"You said twenty minutes, it's only been ten!"

"I know. Do you have some shoes I could borrow?" She could swear she heard Kenzie audibly perk up at that.

"What kind?" Kenzie asked and popped her head into the room.

"Uh, black. Formal," Addy said.

"Well, duh. Hold on."

She listened to Kenzie rush to her bedroom and start to bang around in the closet. Kenzie was half a size smaller than her, but she could handle pinched feet for a few hours.

"These or these?" Kenzie asked. Both were at least six inches.

"Oh, lord, Kenzie. I guess the ones without the platforms."

Kenzie shrugged and tossed the heels onto the bed.

―――

HER SISTER LOOPED her arm through hers as they arrived at the small, Unitarian chapel at the crest of the cemetery's hill. Immediately, virtual strangers swooped down on them to offer their condolences. Some were vaguely familiar to Addy, but most she didn't recognize at all.

"Did Dad really know all these people?" she whispered to Kenzie.

Her sister shrugged.

"Addison, Kenzie, I'm so sorry for your loss." An ancient woman with blue-tinted hair approached them. "My late husband and I simply adored that restaurant when it first opened. Every Sunday, we went—"

Addy listened to the woman drone on as more strangers approached them, offered stiff hugs, and dished up memories of her parents that didn't resonate with her at all.

When the host asked if anyone would like to say any words, Addy held her breath. When nobody stood up, the host turned to her.

"Let's just move to the service," she said.

A staff member whisked them to the graveside in a small golf cart. The simple casket hovered above an open grave with an arrangement of white lilies draped on top.

In lieu of a religious service, Addy had asked that a poem be read. It was the same one their dad's best man had read aloud at their parents' vow renewal all those years ago.

She had been ten years old when they renewed their vows lakeside, and remembered how strange she thought the poem was at the time. Now, Li-Young Lee's "Braiding" finally made sense.

Addy had held it together for the past five days. She hadn't cried once after they'd left the hospital, paralyzed in strength for Kenzie. But as the host read the poem in his soothing voice, she felt the saltwater slip down her cheeks and pool at the corners of her mouth.

Addy let out a quiet sob. Kenzie squeezed her arm gently, and a burst of heat warmed her to the bone from her other side. She felt Jack before she saw him—he didn't have to say anything.

The host continued reading the poem.

Jack took her hand that wasn't intertwined with Kenzie's. His heat, his presence, pushed her over the edge. Finally, Addy felt that she didn't have to carry the burden alone, to be strong enough for both her and Kenzie.

She let the tears fall freely, turned to Jack and buried herself in his dark suit jacket.

———

Addy hadn't even faltered when Kenzie had reached for her car keys. She pushed them into her sister's hands and trusted she would be surrounded by throngs of people who hoisted homemade casseroles at her.

For Addy, the post-funeral feast at home wasn't possible. She'd given up all she could.

Her father was gone. What did it matter if she made small talk between bites of egg salad sandwiches?

Jack drove them back to the condo in silence. His hand rested on her thigh, loving without the raw sexuality that had bound them together for the past few weeks.

When she walked inside his condo, it felt right. It felt like coming home. And that was what made it so hard.

"We can't be together," she said as he came up from behind and wrapped his arms around her.

"I think it's best to not make any serious plans one way or the other at the moment," Jack murmured in her ear.

"I'm serious, Jack," she turned around. "It's got nothing to do with… today."

"Then what is it?"

"It's us! You, you're a world traveler. An adventure junkie. And I'm so not."

"So what?" he asked. "If I wanted to date myself—"

"So I can't hold you back from that. I won't."

"Addy." He took her chin in his hand and tipped her head up. She'd kicked off Kenzie's insane heels as soon as she walked through the door. Barefoot, she felt tiny and safe in his arms. "You're a world traveler, too."

"Jack, be serious—"

"You are. You just don't know it yet."

"I can't—"

"You can. I asked you once what was keeping you here,

remember? It was the restaurant, your dad, Kenzie. If it's the restaurant you were worried about, guess what? You don't owe anything to anyone. Sell it, give it to Kenzie if she wants it, it's not your responsibility anymore."

"And neither is my dad," she said bluntly.

"I didn't say that."

"But you were thinking it."

"So what if I was? It's true. And Kenzie's a big girl. She'll figure it out. She needs to stumble without you there to catch her if she's going to grow up."

"Yeah," Addy said slowly. "I know."

"If you know, then say yes."

"Yes to what?" she asked. Addy probed his eyes with hers.

"To the future."

"I don't know. You're not just an adrenaline junkie. You're hardcore, beyond anything I've seen before. The money doesn't help," she said pointedly.

"Okay, you got me there. If this adventure stuff really bothers you, I'll try to tone it down. I can't make any promises, but I'll try. And that's something, isn't it?"

"Yeah," she said, tearing up. "That's something."

"Come here," he said, wrapping her in his arms. "I love you. You do know that, don't you?"

"And I love you. I really, honestly do," she sighed. "Even today, when I'm overwhelmed with grief. Even when you make me mad."

"I'll repeat myself, then. Just say yes. That's all you have to do."

He stared down at her, his eyes shining with sincerity. She looked up at him for a long moment, then nodded.

"Yes."

And that was all she had to say. He pressed his lips to hers, and she kissed him back.

Tomorrow, or the next day, they would strip each other down and do unspeakable things. But today she was content to have said the words, just to let him hold her. Today, it was enough.

31

A small pang tugged at her heart as she packed up the last of their dad's belongings. Kenzie dropped the box she'd been working on in a huff.

"Ugh, how could Mom and Dad have so much stuff? It didn't seem like it at the time."

"I guess that's the thing about lives. They accumulate so steadily, you don't even see it happening."

Addy ran her finger across the framed photo of the four of them at Disneyland when Kenzie was just three years old. Addy clutched a massive cotton candy. Their parents grinned at the camera, each in a pair of mouse ears.

"I can't believe it's been a month," Kenzie said. "It still seems weird, but also kind of normal. You know what I mean?"

"I know what you mean."

"And I'm not gonna lie, I thought I'd be kind of sad when the Goodwill people hauled away his recliner but I was so relieved. That thing *stunk*."

"Remember the movers are going to be here at eight in the morning to take the boxes to storage. You'll be here, right?" Addy asked.

Kenzie rolled her eyes. "Yeah, yeah, you've only told me a million times."

"Just making sure."

"Hey, what time is it?" Kenzie asked.

Addy pointedly looked at the clock that hung next to the bookcase. "Fifteen 'til one. Why? You have somewhere to be."

"Fifteen 'til—crap. Hey! I have an idea. Let's go get gelato."

"Gelato? Kenzie, I'm not hungry, why don't you call one of your friends—"

"No, like I'm really craving it. Let's just go, just to the place down the street."

"Just go yourself, I'm going to take a shower—"

"*Please*, Addy. There's no gas in my car. I'll buy."

"I'm not worried about who's going to pay, Kenzie."

"*Please*, Addy."

"Oh my God, okay! What's wrong with you? You better not be pregnant. I swear to God, Kenzie, this better not be a pregnancy craving."

"I'm not preggers, you know I have an IUD."

"Alright, well can I shower first? I'm—"

"No, you look super cute. Like Rosie the Riveter, or whatever she's called."

"I don't care how I look, Kenzie, I feel gross—"

"Just come on, you can shower afterward."

"Wow, okay, but just so you know you've become really demanding now that you're the head of this house."

Kenzie grabbed her hand and dragged her out the door.

"Hold on! Let me lock up." Kenzie shifted from side to side.

"I'm just really hungry," she said.

"Then maybe we should get you something besides gelato," Addy said as she locked the front door.

"No, I only want gelato."

"Youngest child, much?" Addy said under her breath.

Kenzie fell into the passenger seat and slid on her sunglasses.

"Drive faster, Grandma," Kenzie said as Addy drove down the gravel driveway.

"I'm trying not to ding the car if you don't mind."

The historic downtown area was bustling with families and couples—or at least as bustling as the small town could be.

"There's a spot, right there!" Kenzie yelled.

"Okay, I see it! Calm down." Addy parallel parked while Kenzie squirmed next to her, desperate to get out of the car. "This better be some freaking amazing gelato. You're driving me crazy."

"Oh, it is. It totally is."

The second Addy put the car in park, Kenzie was out the door.

"Come on!" she yelled.

"I'm coming!" Addy chased after Kenzie and as they rounded the corner of the little brick building, they almost ran directly into Jack.

"Jack!" Addy said. "I thought you were working today."

"Oh, no, I—"

"You better not tell me you lied just to get out of helping us pack," Addy said jokingly. "Not that I'd really blame you."

"No, I was at the hospital, but I got off early to take care of something."

"Hi, Addy." Rosalie came up from behind Jack.

"Hi…" Addy looked at Jack questioningly.

She hated this. Nothing about Rosalie suggested that she was still into Jack—or him into her—but every time she saw her she was hit by just how gorgeous she was.

"Is that Philip over there?" she asked. Addy shaded her eyes and squinted.

Across the street, Philip lurked by a newspaper dispenser. He seemed to be staring at them, but didn't wave or smile. When Addy finally raised her hand in greeting, he awkwardly returned it.

"It's almost one!" Kenzie said as she looked at her phone.

"Kenzie, calm down about the time, you sound like a cuckoo clock. What's Dawn doing here?" she asked suddenly. "She's supposed to be on the lunch shift!" She spotted Dawn across the street, near Philip, but Dawn refused to look at her.

"Dawn!" she called.

"Hey, leave her alone," Jack said, and grabbed Addy's hand.

"What's going on?" Addy looked from Kenzie, to Jack, to Rosalie.

"Oh, God," Rosalie said. She dropped her blonde head into her hands. "I'm a really, really terrible dancer."

"What?" Across the street, Philip took an old-school boom box out of a duffel bag and put it on the bench.

As Bruno Mars' "Marry You" started to blare, Addy noticed scores of people stream onto the pedestrian-only street in formation. Some she recognized from the hospital, many were regulars at the diner.

"What's going on?" She gripped Jack's hand tighter, but he pushed her away.

Addy felt her face flush neon pink as the flash mob sashayed to the music. Jack mouthed the words, and Rosalie was right—she really was a terrible dancer. The bystanders who weren't in on it stopped and stared open-mouthed. A few of them took out their phones to record it.

Philip flipped off the stereo with a flourish as the song came to an end.

"What is this?" Addy repeated as Jack approached her. He was flushed from the dance, boyishly handsome.

"It's a proposal!" he said. "Weren't you listening?"

"Jack, I—"

"Will you marry me, Addy?" he asked.

Jack dropped to one knee and pulled a Tiffany box from his pocket. He propped it open to reveal a rose gold halo engagement ring with a jaw-dropping center diamond.

Addy looked around.

"But we're already married," she hissed to him.

"Marry me again," he said. "I want to do it over, do it right this time."

"Have a party this time!" Kenzie called from the crowd.

"Jack, is this... I don't understand."

"Addy, I want to travel. I'm not going to give that up. But I only want to travel with you. I need someone, I need you, to help balance me out. You know, plan all the adventures, make sure the itinerary's in shape."

"Sounds like you need a travel agent," she said with a laugh.

"No, I need you."

Addy looked around at the crowd, at their friends with smiles plastered across their faces.

"Is this for real?" she whispered.

"It's for real. Unless you'd rather do Reno again—"

"No," she said quickly, with a laugh. "Not that I remember it, but I'm not sure I want to."

"So say yes."

"You're serious?"

"Of course I'm serious. I love you, Addy. I've loved you for a while. Why wouldn't I want to spend the rest of my life with you?"

"I love you, too," she said as tears began to well in her eyes.

"So that's a yes?"

"That's a yes."

Jack rose to his feet as he slipped the diamond on her finger. It overpowered with ease the fake one she'd worn for the past few weeks and carried a weight with it that anchored her.

His lips met hers and she heard the cheers all around them, but in that moment it was just the two of them. Jack pulled her close and nuzzled into her neck.

"Your first task, plan a wedding."

Addy gulped, but she had to admit that her wheels were already turning.

"Anything, big or small, anywhere you want. No limits," he said. "And task two? Plan the honeymoon."

"You have no idea what you're in for," she whispered.

Addy had held back slightly when it came to her Type-A planning, even in the thick of their fake marriage. Even she didn't know what would spring up with the real deal.

"I think I have an idea," Jack said.

"Hey! So are we going to celebrate, or what?" Philip asked. "I got here early, just so you know. Already some old couple called the cops on me thinking I was some creeper loitering on the corner."

"Uh, sure!" Addy said with a laugh. Kenzie grabbed her hand to examine the ring.

"So much better than the last one," she said. "You can thank me for that."

"Kenzie took me shopping," Jack said with a shrug.

"Yeah, and I *only* want to shop with someone who says the sky's the limit from here on out!" Kenzie said.

"Well, let's celebrate," Rosalie said. "What'll it be?"

"Gelato?" Addy asked.

Kenzie laughed.

"What? You've been talking about it nonstop for the past half an hour!"

"Gelato sounds good," Jack said. "Venezia?"

"Uh, the sign says Alotta Gelato," Addy corrected.

"No! I mean the best gelato is in Venezia, Italy. I have a plane at the hangar and our passports in the car. You want to go?" he asked. "It seats twelve, so if anyone wants to grab their passport and meet us there in an hour, you're welcome."

"Kenzie, can you take care of the restaurant?" Addy asked her with a smile.

"Hell, no! Drive me back to the house, I need my passport."

Addy laughed, then whooped aloud when Jack scooped her off her feet, carrying her toward the car. "Only if you can keep up!"

EPILOGUE - JACK

JACK

*J*ack cleared his throat and re-straightened his bow tie.

He couldn't remember the last time he was nervous. But here, in the Archbasilica of St. John Lateran as he waited for Addy to walk down the aisle, he felt like his heart was about to leap out of his chest. The fairytale cathedral was decadently decorated in bouquets and wreaths from the local florist.

Jack could still remember how much he'd struggled to get Addison to indulge in the wedding plans. He watched the guests continue to file in as he hovered near the front of the church.

At first, Addy was adamant that she just wanted a small affair. Maybe a backyard wedding at her parents' old house or the little cottage-style church in town.

"Since when are you so religious?" he'd joked.

Addy had slapped at him.

"All little girls dream of getting married in a church in a white dress. I don't hear you complaining that I'm not a virgin, either."

"You got me there."

As he'd watched her start to put together a tiny, quaint wedding at the local church, he'd genuinely thought it was what she'd wanted. Until he caught her watching the wedding scene in *Made of Honor* with the elegant castle.

"What are you watching?" he'd asked, even though he knew.

Addy had jumped at the sight of him.

"You scared me! Nothing, just some movie."

"Addy, I've heard the same wedding scene playing from the kitchen for the past twenty minutes."

"Okay, fine," she sighed. "Just indulging in some fantasy."

"Why does it have to be a fantasy?"

After a month of encouragement, he finally convinced her to at least consider an extravagant wedding. Of course, the final choice was no surprise.

Italy was the first country they'd visited together, their first trip as a genuinely engaged couple, and the first long plane ride Addy had ever taken.

"Jack, hey! This is amazing."

Philip approached with Rosalie at his side. The two of them had their fingers languidly intertwined. Jack smiled at the new couple. He and Addy had gossiped about it during their international gelato trip, the way Philip teased Rosalie and how around him she finally let her guard down.

The two of them had never made a formal announcement, but their coupledom had been naturally accepted without the need for words.

"This is what happens when you force a limitless budget on the Queen of Planners," he said.

"Did Addy tell you I went with her for her final fitting? You'll be amazed. I'm sure you know that anyway, but seriously, Jack," Rosalie said. "She didn't do too shabby with your tux, either."

"Actually, this was my doing."

"Really? I'm impressed," Rosalie said. "You really have grown up. I remember when we went to that posh restaurant back in the Congo, and you demanded to wear board shorts with a jacket."

"Yeah. Maybe I was kind of a jackass back then."

"Maybe so. I'm glad you've outgrown it," Rosalie said with a smile.

"Is nobody going to comment on my suit?" Philip asked.

"Phil, your suit is from Men's Wearhouse. It's totally fine, but we're in a castle in Italy for what has to be a multi-million-dollar wedding. Nobody's looking at you." Rosalie elbowed him in the ribs to let him know she was joking.

The Italian Symphony, seated overhead in the balcony, began the first strings of "Rondeau from Sinfonies de Fanfares." Rosalie looked up.

"Addy didn't tell me about that."

"That's a surprise from me," Jack said. "Think I did good?"

"She's going to love it."

Addy had asked the event planner to section off the sprawling cathedral to keep the ceremony small and intimate. No matter how much Jack had pushed, she'd stuck to her guns about the size of the guest list—and the lack of a wedding party.

"It's not about the money," she'd told him. "Why would I want to invite people neither of us have seen or talked to in years?"

The planner had done an impeccable job. Gauzy white curtains were intertwined with yellow lights and framed by floor-to-ceiling velvet curtains. With just fifty guests, nobody could tell that it wasn't exactly how the church was meant to look.

Instead, with yards of creamy silk fabric stretched across the pews and punctuated with bouquets, it simply looked like it happened to be the perfect size venue for their wedding.

Second wedding, Jack thought with a smile.

"So, what other surprises do you have in store?" Rosalie asked.

"Excuse me?"

"Come on, Jack, I know you that well. What tricks have you got up your sleeve?"

"You'll just have to wait and see," he said.

Rosalie rolled her eyes and pulled at Philip's arm. They wandered toward the walking cocktail waiters who balanced crystal flutes filled with Armand de Brignac Brut Rosé champagne on silver platters.

From the curtains, he saw Kenzie jet toward Rosalie and take her hand. Kenzie was in the closest thing to a bridesmaid's dress Addy had compromised on—at Kenzie's insistence of course.

"I only have one sister! It might be my only chance to be a maid of honor," Kenzie had pouted when Addy had dropped the bombshell about no wedding party.

"Maybe if you stopped hooking up with your friends' boyfriends after they broke up, that wouldn't be the case!" Addy had laughed.

"It's not like I hook up with them when they're together!" Kenzie had moaned. "Some of them even give permission and then they act all pouty. Hypocrites."

"C'mon, Kenzie, even I know the girl code."

He watched as Kenzie grabbed a glass for herself as she ushered Rosalie into the back where Addy was being pampered, groomed, and put together by a team of Italian stylists. Already, he knew what it was all about. Rosalie was the only one of them who spoke Italian.

Kenzie nearly tripped and fell in her couture Alexander McQueen dress that dripped with Swarovski crystals. He'd given Kenzie permission to not only choose her own dress, but with his credit card.

"Champagne for the groom?" he halted at the accent, but turned politely to the waitress.

"No thank, I'm—Mum. What are you doing here?"

"I assume my invitation got lost in the mail, but of course I wouldn't miss my son's wedding." His mother stood before him in a prim and perfectly tailored lavender skirt suit. She held out one of the two glasses of champagne. Jack accepted, unsure of her angle.

"Cheers," he said, and raised his glass.

"Jacob," she said after they touched glasses. "You know it's bad luck not to make eye contact after a cheers."

He searched his mother's eyes for some ulterior motive as he sipped the champagne that tasted how he imagined liquid gold should. But he found nothing.

"I just want you to know, you have my blessing. Not that you need it, and not that you want it. But I wanted you to know."

"Thank—thank you. Mum," he said. "I'm sorry I didn't invite you."

"Like I said, I'm sure it just got lost in the mail."

"Did you come alone?" he asked.

"Jacob, of course. And don't give me that look of sympathy. Ever since your father ... well, I'm quite used to making it on my own. Besides," his mother said as she scanned the crowd. "I'm sure I can find some accommodating gentleman to show me around Rome once the festivities are over."

He let out a laugh. "And I thought I got my sense of adventure from Dad."

"Don't be silly, Jacob," she said. "Your father, I loved him with everything in me, but he was such a *planner*. Sometimes it drove me mad, but I was better for it. When we met—did I ever tell you this story?"

"No," he said with a shake of his head.

"When we met, your father had just finished his residency and was on a Peace Corps assignment in Cambodia."

"Wait, what? You met in Cambodia?"

"Indeed," she said as she took a long pull of her champagne.

"What ... what were you doing in Cambodia?"

"Surfing, mostly," she said with a shrug. "I was on the mainland from Bamboo Island on a palm wine run—"

"Wait, you need to back up. What are you talking about?"

His mother gave him a smile.

"I lived a whole life before you were even born, Jacob," she said. "I wasn't always the stuffy old woman you know me as now. When your father met me, we were at the same tuk-tuk looking for local liquor. He heard my Melbourne accent and told me, 'Love your dreadlocks, love.' And that was it."

She shrugged nonchalantly.

"Mum, you—"

She wrinkled her nose.

"This isn't classical," she said as she gazed up at the symphony orchestra. "What is this?"

"Bruno Mars."

"Where's that?"

He laughed. "Who, Mum. Here, let me take you to your seat. It means the bride's coming."

Jack seated his mother in the first row and took his position at the end of the aisle. The curtains spread at the far end and his heart soared in his chest.

Addy emerged with her long hair flowing behind her, draped in an exquisite wedding gown with handstitched French lace, long sleeves, and a boat neckline highlighted with gold beads.

The whole room collectively seemed to hold their breath.

EPILOGUE ADDY

ADDY

"I need to sit down," Addy said.

When she'd first walked into the dressing area of the cathedral, it had seemed so big. Even with the makeup artist, hairstylist, seamstress, and the two waiters reserved just for the private area, it was spacious.

But in the custom couture gown heavy with beads and the twelve-foot train behind her, she started to sweat.

"*Che cosa?*" the stylist asked.

"Sit! I need to sit," Addy said. The stylist looked at her in confusion.

"I have Rosalie!" Kenzie said as she rushed into the room.

"What's wrong? What is it?" Rosalie asked.

"I feel dizzy, I need to sit."

"*Lei deve sedersi,*" Rosalie said in perfect Italian to the stylist.

"No!" cried the seamstress. "*Il vestito rugge—*"

"It's fine," Rosalie told the squat woman. "She's worried you'll wrinkle the dress."

With Kenzie's help, Rosalie helped Addy sit carefully in the plush wingback chair. The seamstress tsked and walked away.

"Here, have some juice," Kenzie said, and pushed a glass into her hand. "But don't spill."

"Thanks," Addy said and took a swallow. "Ugh, Kenzie, this is wine. I told you no alcohol until after the ceremony."

"Sorry, but it is juice. Just fermented. It's like ten thousand a bottle and I thought it would help."

"You can't waste that," Rosalie said.

"Fine." Addy downed the glass in one pull. She had to admit, it did calm her.

"No more, though," she said. "I want to remember everything. This time. So, how's it going out there?"

Rosalie's phone buzzed and she checked her messages.

"It's ... good ..."

"Rosalie."

She sighed. "Philip just texted me. Jack's mom is here."

"His *mom* is here? Kenzie, get me another glass."

"*Don't*," Rosalie said as Kenzie sprung up. "But he says it looks like everything's going well. Hold on, he's going to eavesdrop."

The three of them waited in silence while the stylist fussed with Addy's hair. There was so much hairspray she prayed nobody would light a match close to her.

"Oh my God," Rosalie said as she read the message. She let out a laugh.

"What? What is it!" Addy demanded.

"Apparently his mom's getting all sentimental. She gave her blessing, and now she's telling Jack how she met his dad..."

"And?"

"Well, it seems like she was slumming it on the beaches in Cambodia buying palm wine from a shack when his dad fell in love with her dreadlocks."

"You've got to be kidding."

"Look!" Rosalie handed Addy her phone.

"Unbelievable. And she had a problem with me being a waitress."

"Okay, well, I think you're doing better," Rosalie said. "You still need me in here? I can stay, but I thought, maybe... you two would want..."

"Yeah, we're fine," Addy said with a smile. "Thanks."

"Okay. See you out there," Rosalie said with a grin.

"Better?" Kenzie asked.

"Yeah," Addy said after a pause. "I am."

"See? The wine worked."

They listened to the music segue into "The Blue Danube."

"Funny," Addy said. "I told Jack classical music, but this is really good. God, it sounds... heavenly."

Kenzie gave her a funny smile but said nothing.

"Hey, I know you said no more alcohol until after the ceremony, but you need to take two sips."

"What for?" Addy asked.

"One for Mom and one for Dad."

"Do we pour the rest of it on the floor gangster style afterward?" Addy asked.

"No! No champagne on floor!" the event coordinator appeared from the back room.

"There she is, right when you don't need her," Kenzie muttered. She took two glasses from the gold platter and handed one to Addy.

"To Mom," Addy said as they clinked glasses.

"She would have worn a pink dress," Kenzie said. "Like in their vow renewal. Maybe even the same one."

"She could have given me my something borrowed," Addy said with a twinge of sadness.

"You don't like my pantyhose?" Kenzie asked.

"They're great, Kenzie. What I always dreamed my something borrowed to be."

"Don't get all haughty or I won't give you your real something borrowed."

"Excuse me?"

"Here." Kenzie reached into her little beaded purse and pulled out a gold bracelet.

"What is—wait, I remember this. It was Mom's," Addy said.

"She wore it on her wedding day to Dad," Kenzie said with a shrug. "It's what she left me when she... anyway, it's been in a safe deposit box since then, but I figured you could borrow it for today. Considered it borrowed from me and Mom both."

"*No pianto,*" the makeup artist warned sternly. Addy didn't need a translator to figure out *pianto* meant crying.

"I won't," she said quickly.

"Cheers to Dad," Kenzie said, and held up her glass.

Addy forced the tears back inside as she sipped the champagne. Kenzie helped her attach the delicate clasp of the bracelet on her wrist.

"What would Dad have been doing?" Addy asked.

"Honestly? Loving the champagne, probably," Kenzie said.

"Kenzie!"

"What? Too soon? Okay, fine," she said. "He probably would have been embarrassing Mom somehow. Bad Italian accent or something."

"No, she'd just be pretending to be embarrassed," Addy said.

"Yeah, you're right," Kenzie agreed.

The first swells of Bruno Mars' "Marry You" seeped into the room.

"Now you go," the event coordinator said. Kenzie rolled her eyes at Addy.

"Is this Bruno Mars?" she asked. "I told him I wanted 'Canon in D Major!'"

"You want me to change?" the event coordinator asked, her hand already on the walkie-talkie like it was a revolver.

"No," Addy said with a laugh. "No, it's fine. It's perfect, actually."

Kenzie gathered up the train behind her. "Jesus, this weighs like fifty pounds!"

"Don't complain to me. You're not the one who has to have it strapped to your wrist for the reception."

She listened to the click of Kenzie's sky-high heels behind her as the event coordinator took her arm and guided her toward where the curtains parted at the end of the aisle. Through the filmy gauze, she could make out just shapes of people.

Addy's heart began to pound against her ribs.

"I don't think I can do this," she said.

"You do it," the event coordinator said brusquely.

"I'll handle this," Kenzie said, and firmly pushed the coordinator aside. "Addy, what's wrong?"

"I don't... this is all too much," she said.

"You don't have to do anything you don't want to," Kenzie said. "But, remember, you're already married."

That's right. Addy's breathing started to return to normal. The heat from the heavy dress began to lift and radiate out the completely backless dress.

Hold your shoulders proud, she reminded herself. The gown had been designed to be stunning, yet modest from the front and shockingly bare from the back.

"Addy? Are you listening to me?" Kenzie asked.

"I'm already married."

"That's right! So what's the big deal? It's just a party. A crazy expensive party that's already paid for and you're in a crazy expensive dress that you'll only get to wear once. Unless you become one of those loony old ladies that wears her wedding dress for fun."

Addy laughed. "You're right. What's the big deal?"

"You go now," the coordinator said again.

Addy couldn't tell if it was a question or a statement, but the olive-skinned Italian woman parted the curtains and Kenzie moved behind her to gather the train.

As Addy moved through the parted curtains, the images swam before her eyes. Familiar faces stood and beamed smiles at her. The photographer they'd met with for months, who they flew in from Tahoe, discreetly followed her while his team covered other angles.

Addy made it halfway up the aisle before she caught sight of Jack. He stood on the thick marble steps just a few strides away, dashing in his custom suit. But that wasn't what mattered. All that mattered was how he looked at her—like she was the most glorious thing he'd ever seen.

"I'd say you look gorgeous, but that doesn't even come close," he said as she approached. He lightly touched the gemstone-encrusted birdcage veil that covered a sliver of her face. "So, I'll ask you a question instead. Do you like the band?"

"What?"

Jack gestured upward and Addy gasped when she saw the throngs that made up the symphony. "You're crazy," she said.

The rest of the ceremony went by in a blur. Addy remembered saying "I do" and she remembered the kiss, but the rest was so fast.

Maybe you never really remember a wedding, she thought.

EPILOGUE - THE WEDDING
THE WEDDING

The reception in the castle's largest ballroom had started to wind down. Part of Addy was sad to see the party come to an end—but she had to admit her shoes were killing her.

That's what you get for letting Kenzie insist on Louboutins, she thought. She and Jack were both tipsy on champagne, but far from blackout drunk.

"Addison, dear," his mother said as soon as they'd made their grand reception entrance as husband and wife. "I want to apologize about my behavior the last time we met. I was—well, forget it. There's no excuse. I'm just sorry."

"It's... umm... thank you," Addy said.

"I know I don't know you well, but I hope we can change that. You will bring her to Melbourne, won't you, Jacob?"

"Sure, Mum, we'll plan on it." His mother gave them both hugs and kisses on the cheek. As she wandered off, Addy watched her take the arm of a handsome older Italian man.

"Who's that?" Addy asked.

Jack glanced over. "Who knows?"

Addy laughed. As they sat at the sweetheart table, before empty plates of cake, Addy swiped a finger across the frosting and brought it to her tongue.

"Still hungry?" Jack asked with a laugh.

She shrugged. "When your cake is coated in twenty-four-karat gold dusting, you eat all you can!"

"Just don't get too full," he said as he leaned in. "I have plans for you tonight, Mrs. Stratton."

She removed her finger slowly from her lips.

"It's not a legal marriage until it's consummated," she said. "So, technically, we're not married yet."

"Except that we've already been married for months."

"I don't know if a marriage is legal if you can't remember it, though. Maybe Reno never counted."

"So you're saying tonight's the first official night that I'll have you as husband and wife?"

"If you're lucky," she said with a wink. The symphony started the first strains of "Canon in D Major." "Finally!" Addy said.

"I made a few changes," Jack said. "This is the last dance."

"Really?" Even though her feet ached and she was on a sugar high, knowing it was the last moments of their wedding was melancholy.

"Can I have this dance, Mrs. Stratton?"

"If you don't mind me being barefoot."

"I love it," he said.

The other couples joined them on the dance floor. Addy caught a glimpse of Rosalie with her head on Philip's shoulder, Jack's mom with her sudden dark and handsome escort—and Kenzie making out with one of the bartenders as they clutched each other close.

Addy sighed and leaned against Jack's chest. As the last measures of music played, the couples began to part but Jack held her tight for an extra beat. "Now the fun part," he said.

"What's that?"

"Let the honeymoon begin."

"You didn't think this was fun?" she asked coyly.

"Well, sure. I like weddings. But they're not honeymoon fun."

She punched him lightly in the chest as they headed toward the exit. A series of limousines waited to whisk the guests away to hotels. "I have a surprise for you," Addy said.

"What's that?"

"We're not staying at the same hotel as everyone else."

"We're not? But that's where our things are—"

"What's this? Is Mr. Adventure concerned that his plans changed?" she teased.

"*No*, I just thought—"

"I just thought The St. Regis would be a better choice for tonight."

"The St. Regis. You got a room at The St. Regis?" he asked, impressed.

"The honeymoon suite, to be exact. I figured the last thing we needed was to get interrupted in the morning with our friends—okay fine, Kenzie—knocking on our door for breakfast."

"You really do think of everything," he said, and leaned down to kiss her as they waved the last guests off.

"I was just thinking that I didn't want to get cheated out of my morning sex," she said with a shrug.

"Wow, you're pretty confident!"

"You have no idea," she said as she bit her lip and looked up at him.

Their white limo arrived at the tail end of the sea of black limos. Jack helped her down the marble staircase while she delighted in the cool stone against her feet.

"The St. Regis?" the driver asked in a syrupy thick accent.

Addy nodded and let both Jack and the driver help her in. "I might need to sit up front, what with this train!" Jack said.

"Be quiet and get back in here!"

The limo had barely pulled away before Jack raised the partition.

"I've been waiting all night for this," he said.

She felt his hands on her bare back and immediately broke out in shivers. Jack's tongue trailed from her mouth along her jawline as he gently tugged the fabric forward. All he had to do was release her arms and the bodice would fall down with ease.

Addy ached for him, but the desire to draw out the night was stronger.

"No," she panted.

"What's wrong?"

She pushed him away gently. "I'm not that kind of girl," she said and shook her finger at him. "You'll have to wait."

Jack looked at her in exasperation. "If I had any idea how to get this thing off without drowning one of us in the fabric..."

"Be patient," she said.

The limo pulled to a stop and Addy tried her best to clean up her smeared lipstick as the driver opened the door.

"Oh, wow," she said as she gazed up at the nineteenth-century palace. "I saw the photos, but I didn't expect—Jack!" She let out a small shriek as he lifted her into his arms.

"What's the room number?" he asked. "We don't have our own threshold here so this will have to do. Hey, I think all that cake you ate made you put on a few pounds. Or is it the dress?"

"It's the dress," she said with a laugh.

"You're giving me a workout. Room number, quick."

The front desk gave them big grins as Jack nearly ran with her toward the gilded elevators. Addy pulled the room key from her purse and struggled with the heavy wooden door while Jack cradled her in his arms.

As he carried her across the threshold, she gasped. The room was absolutely covered in red rose bouquets while petals were strewn on every surface.

"What kind of package did you ask for?" he asked.

"The honeymoon package, but I didn't expect—"

Jack tossed her on the plush bed while the scent of rose wafted over her.

"Where's the instruction manual?" he asked.

"Pull here, gentle," she said, and she gripped the wrist hem of her dress. The heavy bodice fell into her lap.

Jack let out his breath at the sight of her, bare breasts and an Italian tan.

"Not so fast," she said with a smile. Addy stood up and turned her back to him. "Unzip."

She felt his hands at the zipper, right in between the low dimples of her back. When he lowered it, it fell to the floor. Addy wore nothing but a white thong and a jeweled blue garter high on her thigh.

"Come here." Jack turned her around and lifted her over his shoulder.

"Jack!"

"You teased me enough," he said. "Time for my revenge."

She laughed as he carried her through the spacious suite into the marble covered bathroom. The oversized shower with the multiple rainfall showerheads came to life.

Jack stripped off his own suit and followed her into the shower. She lifted her face to his kisses, to the soft and warm water that fell down on them, and felt his finger hook through the thin panties that she still wore.

"You won't be needing these anymore," he said. He lowered to his knees and kissed his way across her mound and down one thigh as he lowered the thong to the floor.

Addy giggled as he turned her around and pressed on her back. She leaned forward against the glass, her ass presented to him. Jack moved to her other leg and kissed his way up.

The feel of his tongue on her, the spray of the water, the room, the wedding—it all got her wetter than she'd ever been. She let out a moan and parted her legs to offer more access.

Jack buried his face between her cheeks. His tongue probed her opening before it trailed to her rim. She felt his hand between her thighs, his forefinger on her clit.

Addy groaned into the echo of the bathroom, her nipples pressed against the cool glass of the shower wall.

"Does this count as consummation?" Jack asked.

"I think that varies by state," she said.

"Well, we'd better be certain, then." Jack raised to his feet, gripped her shoulders and entered her from behind.

Addy gasped as he filled her.

"Jack," she whispered.

"I love you," he responded as he leaned down to kiss her neck.

"And I love you," she whispered.

GET A FREE BOOK!

Join my mailing list to be the first to know of new releases, free books, special prices and other author giveaways.

http://freehotcontemporary.com

ALSO BY JESSA JAMES

Bad Boy Billionaires
Lip Service
Rock Me
Lumber Jacked
Baby Daddy
Billionaire Box Set 1-4

The Virgin Pact
The Teacher and the Virgin
His Virgin Nanny
His Dirty Virgin

Club V
Unravel
Undone
Uncover

Cowboy Romance
How To Love A Cowboy
How To Hold A Cowboy

Beg Me
Valentine Ever After
Covet/Crave
Kiss Me Again
Handy
Bad Behavior
Bad Reputation

ABOUT THE AUTHOR

Jessa James grew up on the East Coast but always suffered a severe case of wanderlust. She's lived in six states, had a variety of jobs and always comes back to her first true love – writing. Jessa works full time as a writer, eats too much dark chocolate, has an iced-coffee and Cheetos addiction, and can't get enough of sexy alpha males who know exactly what they want – and aren't afraid to say it. Dominant, alpha-male insta-luv is her favorite to read (and write).

Sign up HERE for Jessa's Newsletter:

http://jessajamesauthor.com/mailing-list/

www.ingramcontent.com/pod-product-compliance
Lightning Source LLC
LaVergne TN
LVHW011816060526
838200LV00053B/3802